The Bobbsey Twins On A Houseboat

To order additional copies, please contact us.
BookSurge, LLC
www.booksurge.com
1-866-308-6235
orders@booksurge.com

The Bobbsey Twins On A Houseboat

Laura Lee Hope

BookSurge Classics
Title No. 926
2004

The Bobbsey Twins On A Houseboat

Chapter I

Good News

"What are you doing, Freddie?" asked Bert Bobbsey, leaning over to oil the front wheel of his bicycle, while he glanced at his little brother, who was tying strings about the neck of a large, handsome dog.

"Making a harness," answered Freddie, not taking time to look up.

"A harness?" repeated Bert, with a little laugh. "How can you make a harness out of bits of string?"

"I'm going to have straps, too," went on Freddie, keeping busily on with his work. "Flossie has gone in after them. It's going to be a fine, strong harness."

"Do you mean you are going to harness up Snap?" asked Bert, and he stood his bicycle against the side of the house, and came over to where Freddie sat near the big dog.

"Yes. Snap is going to be my horse," explained Freddie. "I'm going to hitch him to my express wagon, and Flossie and I are going to have a ride."

"Ha! Ha!" laughed Bert. "You won't get much of a ride with that harness," and he looked at the thin cord which the small boy was winding about the dog's neck.

"Why not?" asked Freddie, a little hurt at Bert's laughter. Freddie, like all small boys, did not like to be laughed at.

"Why, Snap is so strong that he'll break that string in no time," said Bert. "Besides--"

"Flossie's gone in for our booty straps, I tell you!" said Freddie. "Then our harness will be strong enough. I'm only using string for part of it. I wish she'd hurry up and come out!" and Freddie glanced toward the house. But there was no sign of his little sister Flossie.

"Maybe she can't find them," suggested Bert. "You know what you and Flossie do with your books and straps, when you come home from school Friday afternoons--you toss them any old place until Monday morning."

"I didn't this time!" said sturdy little Freddie, looking up quickly. "I--I put 'em--I put 'em--oh, well, I guess Flossie can find 'em!" he ended, for trying to remember where he had left his books was more than he could do this bright, beautiful, Saturday morning, when there was no school.

"I thought so!" laughed Bert, as he turned to go back to his bicycle, for he intended to go for a ride, and had just cleaned, and was now oiling, his wheel.

"Well, Flossie can find 'em, so she can," went on Freddie, as he held his head on one side and looked at a knotted string around the neck of Snap, the big dog.

"I wonder how Snap is going to like it?" asked Bert. "Did you ever hitch him to your express wagon before, Freddie?"

"Yes. But he couldn't pull us."

"Why not?"

"'Cause I only had him tied with strings, and they broke. But I'm going to use our book straps now, and they'll hold."

"Maybe they will--if you can find 'em--or if Flossie can," Bert went on with a laugh.

Freddie said nothing. He was too busy tying more strings about Snap's neck. These strings were to serve as reins for the dog-horse. Since Snap would not keep them in his mouth, as a horse does a bit, they had to go around his neck, as oxen wear their yokes.

Snap stretched out comfortably on the grass, his big red tongue hanging out of his mouth. He was panting, and breathing hard, for he and Freddie had had a romping play in the grass, before quieting down for the horse-game.

"There, Snap!" Freddie exclaimed, after a bit. "Now you're almost hitched up. I wish Flossie would hurry up with those straps."

Freddie Bobbsey stood up to look once more toward the house, which his little twin sister had entered a few minutes before, having offered to go in and look for the book straps. She had not come back, and Freddie was getting Impatient.

At last the little girl appeared on the side porch. Her yellow hair blew in the gentle June breeze, making sort of a golden light about her head.

"Freddie! Freddie!" she cried. "I can't find 'em! I can't find the book straps anywhere!"

"Why, I put 'em--I put 'em--" said Freddie helplessly, trying to remember where he had put them, when he came in from school the day before.

"You've got to come and help me hunt for 'em!" Flossie went on. "Mamma says she can't find the straps."

"All right. I'll come," spoke Freddie. "Snap, you stay here!" he ordered, but the big dog only blinked, and stuck out his tongue farther than ever. Perhaps he had already made up his mind what he would do when Freddie let him alone.

Off toward the house went the little fat Freddie. He was pretty plump --so much so that his father often called him a little "fat fireman." Freddie was very fond of playing fireman, ever since the time he had owned a toy fire engine. But to-day he had other ideas.

"I'll find those straps," he said, as he toddled off. "Then we'll hitch Snap to my express wagon, and Flossie and I'll have a fine ride. Don't you run away, Snap."

Snap did not say whether he would or not. Flossie, standing on the side porch, waited for her little brother. She was just his age, and only a little smaller in height. She was just about as fat and plump as was Freddie, and both had light curly hair. They made a pretty picture together, and if Freddie was a "fat fireman" Flossie was a "fat fairy," which pet name her father often called her.

"Did you look under the sofa for the straps?" asked Freddie when he had joined his sister.

"Yes. I looked there, and--and--everywhere," she answered. "I can't find 'em."

"Maybe Snap hid 'em," suggested Freddie.

"Maybe," agreed Flossie. "He would, if he knew you were going to hitch him up with 'em."

"Pooh. He couldn't know that," said Freddie. "I

didn't know it myself until a little while ago, and I didn't tell anybody but you."

"Well, maybe Snap heard us talking about it," went on Flossie. "He's awful smart, you know, Freddie, from having been in a circus."

"But he isn't smart enough for that, even if he can do lots of tricks," Freddie went on. "There's Snoop!" he exclaimed, as a big, black cat ran across the lawn. "Maybe she took our book straps."

"She couldn't," said Flossie. "Our books were in 'em, and they'd be too heavy for Snoop to drag."

"That's so," admitted Freddie. "Well, come on, we'll find 'em!"

The twins went into the house and began searching for the straps. High and low they looked, in all the usual, and unusual, places, where they sometimes tossed their books when they came in from school Friday afternoons, with the joyous cry of:

"No more lessons until Monday! Hurray!"

But this time they seemed to have tossed their books and straps into some very much out-of-the-way place, indeed.

"We can't find 'em," said Flossie. "Can't you take some strong string, to tie Snap to the wagon, instead of the straps, Freddie?"

"I don't think so," he answered. "I know what to do. Let's ask Dinah. Maybe she's seen 'em."

"Oh, yes, let's!" agreed Flossie, and together they hurried to the kitchen where Dinah, the big, good-natured, colored cook, was rattling the pots and pans.

"Dinah! Dinah!" cried Flossie and Freddie in a twins' chorus.

"Yep-um, honey-lambs! What yo' all want?" asked Dinah, opening the oven door, to let out a little whiff of a most delicious smell, and then quickly closing it again. "Ef yo' wants a piece ob cake, it ain't done yit!"

"Oh, Dinah! We don't want any cake!" said Freddie.

"What's dat? Yo' don't want cake?" and Dinah quickly straightened up, put her fat hands on her fat hips, and looked at the two children in surprise. "Yo--don't--want--no cake!" gasped Dinah. "What's de mattah? Yo' all ain't sick, is yo'?"

For that was the only reason she could think of why Flossie and Freddie should not want cake--as they generally did Saturday morning.

"No, we're not sick," said Flossie, "and we'd like a piece of cake a little later, please Dinah. But just now we want our book straps. Have you seen 'em?"

"Book straps! Book straps!" exclaimed Dinah in great surprise. "Go 'long wif yo' now! I ain't got no time to be bodderin' wif book straps, when dey's pies an' puddin's an' cakes t' bake. Trot along now, an' let ole Dinah be! Book straps! Huh!"

Flossie and Freddie knew there was little use in "bodderin'" Dinah any more, especially when she was in the midst of her baking.

"Come on, Flossie," spoke Freddie. "We'll have another look for those straps. Next time I'll put our books where we can find 'em."

Once more the children started through the different rooms. They looked everywhere. But no straps could they find.

"You see what a lot of trouble it makes, not only for you, but for others as well, when you don't take care of your books," said Mrs. Bobbsey gently. She knew it would be a good lesson for the twins to search for their things. Next time they might remember.

Suddenly, from out in the yard, came a shout.

"Freddie! Freddie! Come out here, quick!"

"That's Bert!" exclaimed Freddie.

"Oh, maybe he's found the straps, so we can harness up Snap," cried Flossie.

But Bert's next words soon told the younger twins that it was no such good luck as that, for he cried:

"Snap's running away, Freddie! He's running away. If you're going to harness him up you'll have to catch him!"

"Oh dear!" cried Flossie.

"Come on, help me catch him!" called Freddie.

Together they ran into the yard. As Bert had said, Snap, getting tired of being tied to a post with a thin string, had broken the cord, and now was racing over the fields after another dog with whom he often played.

"Come back, Snap! Come back!" cried Freddie.

Snap paid no heed.

Just then, through the front gate, came a girl. She looked so much like Bert, with his dark hair and eyes, with his slimness and his tallness, that you could tell at once she was his sister. As soon as Flossie saw her, she cried:

"Oh, Nan! We were going to hitch Snap to the express wagon, but Freddie and I can't find our straps, and Snap ran away, and--and--"

"Never mind, Flossie dear," said Nan. "Wait until you hear the good news I have for you!"

"Good news?" exclaimed Bert, coming away from his bicycle, toward his twin sister.

"Yes, the very best!" Nan went on. "It's about a houseboat! Now, Flossie and Freddie, sit down on the grass and I'll tell you all about the good news!"

Chapter II

Snap Saves Freddie

Down on the soft green grass of the lawn, sat the two sets of Bobbsey twins. Yes, there were two "sets" of them, and I shall tell you how that was, in a little while.

"Begin at the beginning," suggested Bert to his sister. He always liked to hear all of anything, so Nan prepared to skip nothing.

"Well," said Nan, as she leaned over to re-tie the bow of Flossie's hair ribbon. It had become loose in the hurried search for the book straps. "Well, you know I went down to papa's lumber office this morning, to bring him the letter that came here to the house by mistake. It was a letter from--"

"You can skip that part of it," suggested Bert. "I don't want to wait so long about hearing the news."

"Well, I thought I'd tell you everything," said Nan. "Anyhow, when I was in papa's office he bought it."

"What did he buy?" asked Freddie, getting to the point more quickly than Bert would have done. "What'd he buy, Nan?"

"A houseboat," went on the older girl twin.

Mr. Marvin was there, and he sold papa the Marvin houseboat. Oh! and such fun as we're--"

"What's a houseboat?" interrupted Flossie.

"It's a boat with a house on it, of course," spoke Bert, eagerly. "I know. I've seen lots of them. You can live in them just like in a house, only it's on water. There's more room in a houseboat than in a regular boat. Go on, Nan."

"Are we going to live in it?" asked Freddie.

"I think so--at least part of the time," said Nan. "Now I'll tell you all I know about it. I couldn't stay to ask all I wanted to, as papa was busy. Besides, it was sort of a secret, and I found it out by accident before he meant me to. So you mustn't tell mamma yet--it's to be a surprise to her," and Nan looked at the two smaller twins, and raised a cautioning finger.

"I won't tell," promised Flossie.

"Neither will I," promised Freddie. "Is that all you're going to tell us, Nan?"

"Well, isn't that enough?" demanded Nan. "I think it's just fine, that we're going to have a houseboat! I've always wanted one."

"So have I," spoke Bert. "Go on, Nan! Tell me more about it. How big is it? Is there an engine in it? Where is it? Can we go on board? When is papa going to get it? Is there a room for me in it? I wonder if I can run the engine and steer? How much did it cost?"

"Gracious!" cried Nan, pretending to cover her ears with her hands. "It will take me all morning, Bert, to answer those questions. Please start over again."

"First tell me where I can see the boat," suggested Bert. "I want to go look at it."

"It's down in the lake," said Nan.

"Come on, Flossie," spoke Freddie. "There's Snap coming back now, and maybe we can catch him. Then we'll harness him up. Dinah ought to be done with her baking now, and maybe she can find those straps for us. Here, Snap!"

Flossie and Freddie, being some years younger than Bert and Nan, did not care to hear much more about the houseboat just then. That they were going to have one was enough for them. They were much pleased and delighted, but they had the idea of hitching Snap to the express wagon, and they could not get that out of their minds.

"You go in and ask Dinah to help you look for the straps," directed Freddie to his little sister, "and I'll catch Snap. Here, Snap! Snap!" he called to the dog who had come back into the yard after a romp and frolic with his animal friend.

Snap was glad enough to stretch out on the grass and rest. He was tired from his run. Freddie put his arms around the dog's neck, and laid his head down on the shaggy coat.

"Now you can't run away again," said Freddie, as he pretended to go to sleep, while Flossie toddled into the house once more, to have another look for the missing book straps.

At a little distance from Freddie sat Nan and Bert, talking about the houseboat, and the good times they would have on board. Freddie roused up, and looked toward the house. Flossie had not yet come out.

"It takes her a long time," said the little boy. "We won't have any ride at all, if she doesn't hurry up."

Then Freddie saw something else that attracted his attention. This was Bert's bicycle, leaning now against the side of a shed. Bert was too much interested in the houseboat to want to ride just then.

A new idea came into Freddie's head.

"I'm going to have a ride on Bert's wheel, while I'm waiting for Flossie to come out with the straps," said the little twin chap. "Bert won't care."

Freddie did not take any chances on asking Bert. His elder brother was still busy talking to Nan about the new houseboat. Freddie scrambled to his feet.

"Now you stay there, Snap!" he commanded the big dog, for Snap, ready again for some fun, was anxious to follow his little master. "Lie down, Snap!" ordered Freddie, and Snap again stretched out.

Freddie walked slowly over toward the bicycle. Of course he was too small to ride it in the regular way, with his feet on the pedals, for his little legs were not long enough to reach them. But he could sit on the seat, and Bert had taught him how to steer a little, so that though a bicycle has only two wheels, and will tip over if it is not properly guided, Freddie could manage to ride a little way on it without toppling over, especially if some one put him on and gave him a push, or if he was given a start down a little hill.

"I'm going to have a ride," thought Freddie. "I'll have a little ride, while I'm waiting for Flossie."

Freddie had a velocipede of his own, but that had three wheels instead of two. Freddie thought two wheels were much more fun than three.

"If I can get up on that bicycle, I'll have a nice

ride," murmured Freddie. He looked toward the house. Flossie was not in sight. She had not yet found the straps.

Then Freddie looked toward Bert and Nan. They were still busy talking about the houseboat. They paid no attention to Freddie.

The little twin chap looked around until he had found a small box. By stepping on this he could get up on the seat of the bicycle, which was leaning against the shed. Then Freddie could give himself a little push, and away he would go. There was a little hill leading from where the bicycle stood down to the gate, and into the road. The gate was open.

"Maybe I can even ride down the road a little way," thought Freddie to himself. "That would be great."

It was rather hard work for Freddie to get up on the bicycle from the box, but he managed it. Then he sat on the leather saddle, and took hold of the handle bars. As I have told you, he knew how to steer, even though he could not reach the pedals.

"Here I go!" cried Freddie softly, as he gave himself a little push. Down the hill he went, along the path, straight for the yard gate.

"Oh! I'm going out in the road!" exclaimed Freddie, this time out loud, for he was far enough away from Nan and Bert now.

And into the road he did go, on Bert's bicycle. The wheel was going faster and faster, for Bert had just oiled it and it rode very smoothly.

"This is great!" Freddie cried. "Maybe I can ride all the way to the bridge."

He looked down the road to where a little white bridge spanned a small brook. And then, as Freddie looked, he saw something which made his heart beat very fast indeed. For, coming right toward him, was a team of horses, hitched to a big lumber wagon--it was one of Freddie's papa's own lumber teams, as the little boy could see for himself.

On came the trotting team, pulling the heavily laden lumber wagon, and, worst of all, there was no driver on the seat to guide the horses. They were trotting away all by themselves, and Freddie was out in the road, on the bicycle that was far too big for him,

"Oh dear!" cried Freddie.

Just then he heard Flossie scream. She had come out on the side porch, and she saw the team coming toward her little brother.

"Nan! Bert!" screamed Flossie. "Look at Freddie!"

Nan and Bert jumped up and raced down the path.

"Freddie's in trouble again!" thought Bert.

It was not the first time Freddie had gotten into mischief. Though usually he was a pretty good boy, he sometimes made trouble without intending to.

I have told you there were two sets of Bobbsey twins, and those of you who have read the first book of this series know what I mean by that. The first book is called "The Bobbsey Twins," and in that I told you how the Bobbsey family lived in an eastern city called Lakeport, at the head of Lake Metoka. Mr. Bobbsey was a lumber merchant, and owned a large sawmill, and a yard, near the lake, in which yard were piled many stacks of lumber.

Nan and Bert were the older Bobbsey twins, being past nine, while Flossie and Freddie were about "half-past-five." So you see that is how there were two sets of twins. Nan was a tall, slender girl, with a dark face and red cheeks. Her eyes were brown, and so were her curls. Bert, too, was quite dark, like Nan.

Flossie and Freddie were very light, with blue eyes. They were short and fat, instead of tall and thin. So you see the two sets of twins were very different.

Oh! such good times as the Bobbsey twins had! I could not tell you all of them, if I wrote a dozen books. But some of the good times I have related in the first book. In the second, called "The Bobbsey Twins in the Country," there are more happenings mentioned.

Uncle Daniel Bobbsey, his wife Sarah, and their son Harry lived in the country, at a place called Meadow Brook, and there the twins often went on their vacation.

Uncle William Minturn, and his wife Emily, with their nine-year-old daughter Dorothy, lived at Ocean Cliff. As you might guess, this was on the coast, and in the third book, "The Bobbsey Twins at the Seashore," I have told you of the good times the children had there, how they saw a wreck, and what came of it.

In "The Bobbsey Twins at School" you will find out how they came to get the dog Snap, as a pet. They already had a black cat, named Snoop, but one day, when the twins, with their father and mother, were on a railroad train, something happened, and Snoop was lost.

They found Snap, instead. He was a circus dog,

and--but there, if you want to read of Snap, you must do so in the book about him. I shall tell you this much, though. Snap was a very fine dog, and could do many tricks, and in the end the Bobbseys kept him for a pet, as well as getting back their lost cat Snoop.

When school was over for the winter holidays one year, the Bobbseys went to "Snow Lodge," and in the book of that name I have told you about a queer mystery the twins helped solve while out amid the snow and ice.

Now the Bobbseys were back in their fine house in Lakeport, where Dinah, the fat cook, gave them such good things to eat, and where Sam Johnson, her husband, kept the lawns so nice and green for the children to play on.

Just now Freddie Bobbsey would have been very glad, indeed, to be playing on that same lawn instead of being on his brother's bicycle, rolling toward the team of lumber horses, who were coming straight for him.

"Oh, look at Freddie! Look at Freddie!" screamed Flossie, dropping the two book straps which she had at last found. "Save him, Nan! Bert! Oh, Freddie!"

"I 'clar t' goodness!" exclaimed fat Dinah in the kitchen. "Dem chillens am up t' some mo' trouble!"

"Freddie, steer to one side! Steer out of the way!" shouted Bert, as he ran for the gate. He could not hope to reach his little brother in time, though.

Freddie was too frightened and excited to steer. The bicycle was going fast--faster than he had ever ridden on it before. All he could do was to sit tight, and hold fast to the handle bars.

"Oh, he'll be run over!" cried Nan, as she, too, raced after Bert.

The team, with no driver to guide it, ran faster and faster. Freddie began to cry. And then, all at once, the front wheel of the bicycle ran over a stone, and turned to one side. The handle bars were jerked from Freddie's grasp, and over he went, wheel and all!

Luckily for him, he fell to one side of the road, on the soft grass, or he might have been injured, but, as it was, the fall did not hurt him at all. One of his little fat legs, though, became tangled up in the wire spokes of the front wheel, and Freddie lay there, with the wheel on top of him, unable to get up.

"Oh, Bert! Bert!" screamed Nan.

"Grab him--quick!" shouted Dinah, waddling down the walk. But she was too fat to go fast enough to do any good.

"Roll out of the way, Freddie!" cried Bert.

Freddie was too much entangled in the wheel to be able to move. And, all the while, the lumber team was coming nearer and nearer to him. Would the horses, with no driver at the reins, know enough to turn to one side, or would the wheels roll over poor Freddie and the bicycle?

Nan covered her face with her hands. She did not want to look at what was going to happen.

"I must get there in time to pull him out of the way!" thought Bert, as he ran as fast as he could. But the team was almost on Freddie now.

Suddenly the dog Snap, who had jumped up when he heard the shouts, saw what the danger was. Snap knew about horses, and he was smart enough to know that Freddie was in danger.

Without waiting for anyone to tell him what to do, Snap ran straight for the lumber team. Leaping up in front of them, and barking as loudly as he could, Snap turned the trotting horses to one side. And just in time, too, for, a little more, and one of the front wheels of the heavily loaded lumber wagon would have run over the bicycle in which Freddie was still entangled.

"Bow wow!" barked Snap. The horses were perhaps afraid of being bitten, though Snap was very gentle. At any rate, they turned aside, and would have run on faster, only Snap, leaping up, grabbed the dangling reins in his teeth and pulled hard on them. "Whoa!" called Bert. When the horses heard this, and felt the tug on the lines, they knew it meant to stop. And stop they did. Snap had saved Freddie.

Chapter III

Dinah's Upset

"What's the matter? What has happened?" asked Mrs. Bobbsey, who had run out to the front porch, upon hearing the excited cries, and the exclamations of fat Dinah, the cook. "Oh! has anything happened to any of the children?"

"Yes'm, I s'pects there has, ma'am," said Dinah. "Pore li'l Freddie am done smashed all up flatter'n a pancake, Mrs. Bobbsey!"

"Freddie--Oh!"

"He's all right!" shouted Bert, who had, by this time, reached his little brother, and was lifting him out of the bicycle. "Not hurt a bit, are you, Freddie?"

"N--no, I--I guess not," said Freddie, a bit doubtfully. "I--I'm scared, though."

"Nothing to be frightened at now, Freddie," said Bert, holding up the little chap, so his mother could see him.

"Why, Freddie isn't hurt, Dinah," said Mrs. Bobbsey, in great relief. "What made you think so?"

"Well, I seed him all tangled up in dat two-wheeled velocipede ob Bert's, an' de hoss team was comin' right down on de honey-lamb. I thought shuah he was gwine t' be squashed flatter'n a pancake. But he ain't! Bless mah soul he ain't! Oh, dere's mah cake burnin'!" and into the kitchen ran Dinah, glad, indeed, that nothing had happened worse than the scare Freddie received.

"Good Snap! Good old dog!" said Nan, as she patted his head.

"Bow wow!" barked Snap. He still held the horse reins in his strong white teeth. He was not going to let the horses go yet.

"Oh, Freddie!" cried Mrs. Bobbsey, when she understood what had happened. "What danger you were in! Why did you take Bert's wheel?"

"I--I wanted a ride, Mamma. I didn't think I'd fall off, or that the team would come."

"You must never do it again," said Mrs. Bobbsey. "Never get on Bert's wheel again, unless he is with you to hold you. You are, too small, yet, for a bicycle."

"Yes'm," said Freddie in a low voice.

"But where is the driver of the wagon?" went on Mrs. Bobbsey, looking at the empty seat.

"Maybe he fell off," suggested Nan, who had taken Freddie from Bert, the latter picking up his wheel, and looking to see if it had been damaged by the fall. But it was all right.

"Here comes a driver now," said Flossie, who saw one of the men from her father's lumber yard hurrying along the road.

"Is anybody hurt?" the man asked, as he came up, running and breathing fast, for he had come a long way.

"No one, I think," answered Mrs. Bobbsey. "But my little boy had a very narrow escape."

"I am sorry," said the driver. "I left the team standing out in front of the lumber yard, while I went in the office to find out where I was to deliver the planks. When I came out the horses were trotting away. I guess they were scared by something. I ran fast, but I could not catch them."

"Snap caught them for you," said the twins' mother, as she looked at the former circus dog, who was still holding the horse-reins.

"Yes, he's a good dog," the lumber wagon driver said. "I was afraid, when I saw how far the horses had gone, that they might do some damage. But I'm glad no one was hurt."

"I think we all are glad," spoke Mrs. Bobbsey. "It was partly my little boy's own fault, for he should not have gotten on his brother's bicycle. But he won't do it again."

"No, I never will!" promised Freddie, as he rubbed his leg where it had been bruised a little from becoming tangled up in the wire spokes.

Snap barked and wagged his tail, as the driver took the lines from him, and then, when the man drove off with the horses and the load of lumber, Mrs. Bobbsey went with the twins back into the yard.

"Well, I'm glad all the excitement is over," she said. "Where were you, Nan? Grace Lavine called for you, but I looked out in the yard and did not see you, so she went away again."

"Why, I went down to papa's office, Mamma, with that letter you gave me for him."

"Yes, I know, but I supposed you had come back. What kept you so long?"

"Well, I--er--I was talking to papa, and---"

Nan did not want to go on. for she did not want to tell that she had been talking about the houseboat.

Mr. Bobbsey had been intending to keep that as a little secret surprise for his wife, but now, if her mother asked about it, Nan felt she would have to tell. She hardly knew what to say, but just then something happened that made everything all right.

Mr. Bobbsey himself came hurrying down the street, from the direction of his lumber office. He seemed much excited, and his hat was on crooked, as though he had not taken time to put it on straight.

"Is everything all right?" he called to his wife. "None of the children hurt?"

"No, none of them," she answered with a smile. Mr. Bobbsey could see that for himself now, since Freddie and Flossie were going up the walk together, Freddie tying one of the book straps around the dog's neck, while Nan and Bert followed behind them, with Mrs. Bobbsey.

"Someone telephoned to me," said the lumber merchant, "that they saw one of our teams running away down this street, and I was afraid our children, or those of some of the neighbors, might be hurt. So I hurried down to see. Did you notice anything of a runaway team?"

"Yes," said Mrs. Bobbsey. "But everything is all right now. Only I haven't yet heard what it was that kept Nan so long down at your office," and she smiled.

Nan looked at her father, and Mr. Bobbsey looked at Nan. Then they both smiled and laughed.

"To tell you the truth," said Mr. Bobbsey, with another smile, "Nan discovered a secret I was not going to tell at once."

"A secret?" asked Mrs. Bobbsey in surprise.

"Yes, it's about---" began Nan.

Then she stopped.

"Go on. You might as well tell her," said Mr. Bobbsey, laughing.

"I know!" exclaimed Freddie, who was all over his fright now. "It's about a boathouse and---"

"A houseboat!" interrupted Bert. "You've got the cart before the horse, Freddie."

"That's it!" exclaimed Nan. "Papa has bought the Marvin's houseboat, Mamma, and we're going to have lovely times in it this summer."

"And I'm going to run the engine," declared Bert.

"I'm going to be fireman!" cried fat Freddie. "I'm going to put on coal and squirt water on the fires!"

"I'm going to sit on deck and play with my dolls," spoke Flossie, who was trying to climb up on Snap's back to get a ride.

Mrs. Bobbsey looked at her husband.

"Really?" she asked. "Have you bought the boat?"

"Yes," he replied, "I have. You know we have been thinking of it for some time. Lake Metoka would be just fine for a houseboat, and we could go on quite a cruise with one. Mr. Marvin wanted to sell his boat, and as he and I had some business dealings, and as he owed me some money, I took the boat in part payment."

"And is it ours now, Papa?" asked Bert.

"Yes, the houseboat is ours. It is called the Bluebird,

and that is a good name for it, since it is painted blue--like your eyes, little fat fairy!" he cried, catching Flossie up in his arms.

"Is it a big boat, Papa?" asked Bert. Like most boys he liked things big and strong.

"Well, I think it will be large enough," said Mr. Bobbsey with a smile as he set down Flossie and caught up Freddie in the same way. "Were you frightened when you fell down and saw the lumber team coming toward you?" he asked.

"A little," Freddie said. "But I wished my legs were long enough so I could ride Bert's bicycle. Then I could get out of the way."

"You'd better keep away from the wheel until you are bigger," said his father, who had been told about the accident and the excitement. "But now I must get back to the office. I have plenty of work to do."

"Oh, but can't you stay just a little longer, to tell us more about the boat!" pleaded Nan. "When can we have a ride in it?"

"A boat is called 'her,'" interrupted Bert,

"Well, 'her' then," said Nan. "Tell us about her, papa. I didn't hear much at your office."

"You heard more than I meant you to," said Mr. Bobbsey with a smile. "Nan came in with that letter just as Mr. Marvin and I were finishing our talk about the houseboat," he went on. "I was going to keep it secret a little longer, but it's just as well you should know now.

"I think you will like the Bluebird. It has a little gasoline engine, so we can travel from place to place. And there is a large living room, a kitchen, several bed rooms and a nice open deck, where we can sit, when it is too hot to be inside."

"Oh, that's going to be great!" cried Bert. "I want a room near the engine."

"And can I be a fireman?" asked Freddie.

"I want to be near mamma--and you," spoke little Flossie.

"Oh, isn't it going to be lovely!" exclaimed Nan, clapping her hands.

"Scrumptious, I call it!" cried Bert, and he ran into the house, through the hall, and into the dining-room, just as big, fat Dinah, the cook, was entering the same room, carefully holding a big cake which she had just covered with white frosting.

"Oh dear!" cried Bert, as he ran, full tilt, Into the big cook.

"Good land ob massy!" fairly yelled Dinah. "Wha-
-wha---"

But that was all she could say. She tried to save herself from falling, but she could not. Nor could Bert. He went down, on one side of the doorsill, and Dinah sat down, very hard, on the other, the cake bouncing from her hands, up toward her head, and then falling into her lap.

Chapter IV

At the Houseboat

"Did--did I hurt you, Dinah?" asked Bert, after he had gotten his breath. "I'm--I'm sorry--but did I hurt you?"

"Hurt me? Hurt me, honey lamb? No indeedy, but I done reckon yo' has hurt yo'se'f, honey! Look at yo' pore haid!" and she pointed her fat finger at Bert.

"Why, what's the matter with my head?" he asked, putting up his hand. He felt something sticky, and when he looked at his fingers, he saw that they were covered with white stuff.

"Oh, it's the frosting off the cake!" said Nan with a laugh. "You look something like one of the clowns in the circus, Bert, only you haven't enough of the white stuff on."

"And look at Dinah!" laughed Freddie. "She's turning white!"

"What's dat, honey lamb? Turnin' white?" gasped the big, colored cook. "Don't say dat!"

"It's the cake frosting on Dinah, too!" said Mrs. Bobbsey. "Oh, Bert! why aren't you a little more careful?"

"I'm sorry, mamma," Bert said, as he watched

Dinah wipe the frosting off her face with her apron. "I didn't know she was coming through the door then."

"And I shore didn't see yo', honey lamb," went on the cook. "Land ob massy! Look at mah cake!" she cried, as she gazed at the mass in her lap. "All de frostin' am done slid off it!"

"Yes, you're a regular wedding cake yourself, Dinah," said Mr. Bobbsey, who had come in to see what all the noise meant. "Well, this seems to be a day of excitement. I'm glad it was no worse, though. Better go up stairs and wash, Bert."

"The cake itself isn't spoiled," said Mrs. Bobbsey, lifting it from Dinah's lap, so the colored cook could get up. It was no easy work for her to do this, as she was so fat. But at last, after many groanings and gruntings, she rose to her feet, and took the cake from Mrs. Bobbsey.

"I'll put some mo' frostin' on it right away, ma'am," she said. "An' I hopes nobody else runs inter me," she went on with a laugh. "I shuah did feel skeered dat Bert was hurt bad."

They could all laugh at the happening now, and after Mr. Bobbsey had told a little more about the new houseboat, he went back to the office.

"Come on, Flossie," suggested Freddie. "Now you've found the book straps, we can hitch Snap to the express wagon. Where'd you find 'em?"

"The straps were on our books, under the hall rack," said Flossie.

"That's just where I left 'em!" exclaimed Freddie. "I knew I left 'em somewhere."

"But next time you must remember," cautioned

his mother. "And remember another thing--no more bicycle rides--you stay on your velocipede."

"Yes'm," said Freddie. "Come on, Flossie. Where's Snap?"

When the little twins went to look for their big, shaggy pet, who could do so many circus tricks, they could not find him.

"Have you seen Snap?" asked Freddie of Dinah's husband, Sam Johnson, who was out in the barn.

"Snap?" repeated the colored man. "Why, Freddie, I done jest see Snap paradin' down de road wif dat black dog from Mr. Brown's house."

"Then Snap's gone away again," said Flossie with a sigh. "Never mind, Freddie. Let's play steamboat, and you can be the fireman."

"All right," he agreed, much pleased with this idea. "We'll make believe we're in our new houseboat. Come on."

"Steamboat" was a game the smaller twins often played on the long Saturdays, when there was no school. All they needed was an old soap box for the boat, and some sticks for oars. Then, with some bits of bread or cake, which Dinah gave them to eat, in case they were "shipwrecked," they had fine times.

Meanwhile, Bert and Nan had asked permission of their mother to go over to where some of their boy and girl friends lived, so they were prepared to have a good time, too.

"Oh, but what fun we'll have on the houseboat, won't we, Bert?" said Nan.

"That's what we will," he agreed with a laugh.

Monday morning came, after Sunday (as it always does if you wait long enough) and the two sets of Bobbsey twins started for school.

"I wish we didn't have to go," said Bert, as he strapped up his books. "I want to go down to our new houseboat."

"But you must go to school," said his mother with a smile. "There will not be many more days now. June will soon be over, and you know school closes a little earlier than usual this year. So run along, like good children."

Off they hurried and soon they were mingling with their boy and girl friends, who were also on their way to their classes.

"You can't guess what we're going to have," said Freddie to a boy named Johnnie Wilson, who was in his room.

"Kittens?" asked Johnnie.

"No."

"Puppies?"

"No."

"I give up--what is it?"

"A houseboat," said Freddie. "It's a house on a boat, and you can live in it on water."

"Huh!" said Johnnie. "There isn't any such thing."

"Yes, there is, too, isn't there, Flossie?" and Freddie appealed to his small sister.

"'Course there is," she said. "Our papa bought one, and Freddie's going to be the fireman, and I'm going to cook the meals, so there! Haven't we got a houseboat, Nan?"

"Yes, dear," answered the older sister, who was

walking with Bert. At this, coming from Nan, Johnnie had nothing to say, except that he murmured, as he walked away:

"Huh! A houseboat's nothing. We've got a baby at our house, and it's got hair on its head, and two teeth!"

"A houseboat's better'n a baby," was Freddie's opinion.

"It is not!" cried Johnnie.

"It is so!" Freddie exclaimed.

"Hush!" begged Nan. "Please don't dispute. Houseboats and babies are both nice. But now it's time to go to school."

The Bobbsey twins could hardly wait for the classes to be out that day, for their mother had promised to call for them after lessons, and, with their father, they were going to see the Bluebird. The houseboat had been brought up the lake by Mr. Marvin, and tied to a dock not far from Mr. Bobbsey's lumber office. The boat was now the property of Mr. Bobbsey, but that gentleman had not yet fully planned what he would do with her.

Just as the children were trooping out of the school yard, along came Mrs. Bobbsey. Nan and Flossie saw their mother and hastened toward her, while Freddie and Bert came along more slowly.

In a little while all five of them were at Mr. Bobbsey's lumber office. He came out of his private room, when one of his clerks told him Mrs. Bobbsey and the children were there.

"Ah, what can I do for you to-day?" asked Mr. Bobbsey of his wife, just like Mr. Fitch, the grocery-store-keeper. "Would you like a barrel of sawdust, ma'am; or a bundle of shingles to fry for the children's suppers?" and Mr. Bobbsey pretended he was no relation to his family.

"I think we'll have a houseboat," said his wife with a laugh. "Have you time to take us down to it? I can't do a thing with these children, they are so anxious to see the Bluebird." "Well, I hope they'll like her," said Mr. Bobbsey, "and not pull any feathers out of her tail."

"Oh, is there a real bird on the boat?" asked Flossie.

"No, papa is only joking," said Nan, with a smile.

Mr. Bobbsey put on his hat, and soon the whole Bobbsey family had reached the place where the boat was tied. At the first sight of her, with her pretty blue paint and white trimming, Nan cried:

"Oh, how lovely!"

"And how big it is!" exclaimed Freddie his eyes large and round with wonder.

"Let's go aboard--where's the gang-plank?" asked Bert, trying to use some boat language he had heard from his father's lumbermen.

The Bluebird was indeed a fine, large houseboat, roomy and comfortable. The children went inside, and, after looking around the main, or living room, and peering into the dining-room, Nan opened the door of a smaller compartment. Inside she saw a cunning little bed.

"Oh, may I have this room?" she asked. "Isn't it sweet!"

"Here's another just like it," said Mrs. Bobbsey, opening the next door.

"That will be mine," said Flossie.

"My room's going to be back here, by the engine," spoke Bert, as he picked out his sleeping place.

"And I'll come with you," said Freddie. "I'm going to be fireman!" Gleefully the children were running about, clapping their hands, and finding something new and strange every minute.

"Where is your room, mamma?" asked Nan. "We ought to have let you and papa have first choice."

"Oh, there are plenty of rooms," said Mr. Bobbsey. "Let's go up on deck and---"

He stopped suddenly, and seemed to be listening.

"What is it?" asked his wife.

"There seems to be some one on this boat beside ourselves," answered Mr. Bobbsey. "I'll go look."

Chapter V

The Strange Boy

The Bobbsey twins looked at one another, and then at their mother, as Mr. Bobbsey went out of the living room of the houseboat, toward the stairway that led up on deck.

Bert tried to look brave, and as though he did not care. Nan moved a little closer to her mother. As for Flossie, she, too, was a little frightened, but Freddie did not seem at all alarmed.

"Is it somebody come to take the boat away from us?" he asked in his high-pitched, childish voice. "If it is--don't let 'em, papa."

They all laughed at this--even Mr. Bobbsey, and he turned to look around, half way up the stairs, saying:

"No, Freddie, I won't let them take our boat."

"Pooh! Just as if they could--it's ours!" spoke Bert.

"Who could it be on board here, mamma?" asked Nan.

"I don't know, dear, unless it was some one passing through the lumber yard, who stopped to see what the boat looked like," answered Mrs. Bobbsey. "Papa will soon find out."

The noise they had heard was the footsteps of some one walking about on the deck of the houseboat.

"Perhaps it was one of the men from the office, who came to tell papa he was wanted up there, or that some one wanted to speak to him on the telephone," went on Mrs. Bobbsey. She saw that the children, even Bert, were a little alarmed, for the boat was tied at a lonely place in the lumber yard, and tramps frequently had to be driven away from the piles of boards under which there were a number of good places to sleep.

Mr. Bobbsey did not mean to be unkind to the poor men who had no homes, but tramps often smoke, and are not careful about their matches. There had been one or two fires in the lumber yard, and Mr. Bobbsey did not want any more blazes.

Soon the footsteps of the children's father were heard on the deck above them, and, a little later Freddie and the others could hear the talk of two persons.

"I guess it was one of the men," said Mrs. Bobbsey.

"I'm going to see," spoke Bert, and he moved toward the stairway, followed by Nan, Flossie and Freddie. They went up on deck and saw their father talking to a strange boy. None of the Bobbsey children knew him.

"Are you looking for some one?" asked Mr. Bobbsey kindly, of the strange boy. Often, when he was in distant parts of the lumber yard, and he was wanted at the office, or telephone, his men might ask some boy to run and tell the owner of the yard he was needed. But Mr. Bobbsey had never seen this lad before.

"No, sir, I--I wasn't looking for any one," said the boy, as he looked down at his shoes, which were full of holes, and put his hands into the pockets of his trousers, which were quite ragged. "I was just looking at the boat. It's a fine one!"

"I'm glad you like it," said Mr. Bobbsey with a smile.

"Could you go to sea in this boat?" asked the boy, who was not very much older than Bert.

"Go to sea? Oh, no!" answered Mr. Bobbsey. "This boat is all right on a lake, or river, but the big waves of the ocean would be too strong for it. We don't intend to go to sea. Why? Are you fond of sailing?"

"That's what I am!" cried the boy. "I'm going to sea in a ship some day. I'm sick of farm-life!" and his eyes snapped.

"Are you a farmer?" asked the twins' father.

"I work for a farmer, and I don't like it--the work is too hard," the boy said, as he hung his head.

"There is plenty of hard work in this world," went on Mr. Bobbsey. "Of course too much hard work isn't good for any one, but we must all do our share. Where do you work?"

"I work for Mr. Hardee, who lives just outside the town of Lemby," answered the boy.

"Oh, yes, I know Mr. Hardee," spoke Mr. Bobbsey. "I sold him some lumber with which he built his house. So you work for him? But what are you doing so far away from the farm?"

"Mr. Hardee sent me over here, to Lakeport, on an errand."

"Well, if I were you I wouldn't come so far away from where I left my horse and wagon," cautioned Mr. Bobbsey, for the place where the boat was tied was a long distance from the main road leading from Lakeport to Lemby.

"I didn't come in a wagon," said the boy. "I walked."

"What! You don't mean to say you walked all the way from Lemby to Lakeport?" exclaimed Mrs. Bobbsey, who had now come up on deck.

"Yes'm, I did," answered the boy. "Mr. Hardee said he needed the horses to work on the farm. He said I was young, and the walk would do me good. So Mrs. Hardee, she gave me some bread and butter for my lunch, and I walked. I'm walking back now, and I came this way by the lake. It's a short cut.

"Then I happened to see this boat here. I like boats, so I thought it wouldn't hurt to come on board."

"Oh, no, that's all right!" said Mr. Bobbsey quickly. "I'll be glad to have you look around, though this is only a houseboat, and not built for ocean travel. So you work for Mr. Hardee, eh? What's your name?"

"Will Watson," the boy said. Mrs. Bobbsey was trying to motion to her husband to come toward her. It seemed as though she wanted to say something to him privately.

"Will Watson, eh?" went on Mr. Bobbsey. "I don't seem to know any family of that name around here."

"No, I don't belong around here," the boy said. "I come from out west --or I used to live there when I was littler. I've got an uncle out there now, if I could ever find him. He's a gold miner."

"A gold miner?" said Mr. Bobbsey, and then his wife came up to him, and whispered in his ear. Just what she said the twins could not hear, but, a moment later Mr. Bobbsey said:

"Bert, suppose you take Will down and show him the boat, since he is so interested."

"Oh, I'm going to!" cried Freddie. "I want to show him where I'm going to be a fireman."

"And I want to show him my room," said Flossie.

The strange boy looked at the little twins and smiled. He had a nice face, and was quite clean, though his clothes were ragged and poor.

"Come along down if you like," said Bert kindly. "There's a lot to see below the deck."

With a friendly nod of his head Will Watson followed the three children. Nan stayed on deck with her parents.

"It's a shame to make him walk all the way from Lemby here and back," said Mrs. Bobbsey. "It must be all of five miles each way."

"It is," said Mr. Bobbsey. "Quite a tramp for a little fellow."

"Can't you find some way to give him a ride back?" asked his wife. "Aren't any of your wagons going that way?"

"Perhaps," replied Mr. Bobbsey. "I'll find out, and I'll send him as near to Mr. Hardee's place as I can."

"Poor little fellow," said Mrs. Bobbsey, and she thought how hard it would be if her son Bert had to go to work for his living so young.

"He seems like a nice boy," spoke Mr. Bobbsey,

"and from what I know of Mr. Hardee he isn't an easy man to work for. Well, have you seen enough of the boat, Nan? Do you think you'll like it?"

"Oh, I just love it," Nan answered. "I'm so anxious for the time to come when we can go sailing, or whatever you do in a boat like this. Mamma, may I bring some of my things from home to fix up my room?"

"I think so--yes. We shall have to talk about that later. I think it is time we started home now. Dinah will not want to wait supper for us."

"Well then, run along," said Mr. Bobbsey. "I'll get the others up from down below."

"And you won't forget about trying to give that boy a ride home?" asked Mrs. Bobbsey.

"No, indeed," replied her husband. "I'm going right back to the office now, and I'll take him with me. I'll let him ride on the wagon that's going nearest to Lemby."

Mr. Bobbsey met Bert and the strange boy coming up.

"It sure is a dandy boat!" said Will Watson with a sigh of envy. "If ever I go away to sea, I hope I'll have as nice a room as yours," and he looked at Bert. "I just couldn't help coming on the boat when I saw her tied here," he went on. "I hope you didn't mind."

"Not a bit!" exclaimed Mrs. Bobbsey, wishing she had some of Dinah's cake or crullers with her to give to the boy, for the twins' mother thought he looked hungry.

The door, leading into the cabin of the houseboat was locked, and they all went on shore, over the gangplank, the board that extended from the dock to the boat.

"Good-bye, Bluebird!" called Flossie, waving her fat, chubby, little hand toward the houseboat. "We'll soon be back."

"And I'm going to bring my fire engine, when I come again," exclaimed Freddie. "If the boat gets on fire I can put it out."

"Boats can't get on fire in the water!" declared Flossie.

"They can so--can't they, papa?" appealed the little boy.

"Well, sometimes, perhaps. But we hope ours doesn't," replied Mr. Bobbsey with a smile. He led the way off the boat, and as Will was about to walk on along the lake shore, on his return to Lemby, Mrs. Bobbsey said:

"Wouldn't you like a ride back, little boy?"

"Indeed I would," he said. "My feet hurt, on account of my shoes being so full of holes, I guess. I'm pretty tired, but I had a little rest. I don't expect to get back much before dark."

"Well, perhaps you can ride nearly all the way," went on Mrs. Bobbsey. "My husband has some lumber wagons going in your direction."

"Yes, come along and we'll see what we can do for you," put in the twins' father, nodding at the strange boy.

Will went off with Mr. Bobbsey, while Nan, Bert, Flossie and Freddie walked with their mother.

"Oh, mamma, when do you think we can go in our boat?" asked Flossie.

"Well, as soon as school closes, my dear."

"And will we sail across the ocean?" Freddie wanted to know.

"Of course not!" cried Bert. "A houseboat isn't a ship."

"That boy knew about ships," said Nan. "I like him, don't you, mamma?"

"Yes, he seemed real nice. He hasn't a very easy life, I'm afraid, working on a farm. But we must hurry on to supper. We'll talk about the boat after papa comes home."

Chapter VI

Freddie's Fire Engine

"Papa, when can we go sailing in the houseboat?"

"May I take my fire engine along?"

"Where did you leave that boy?"

"Did he get a ride to Lemby?"

"Thus Bert, Freddie, Flossie and Nan questioned Mr. Bobbsey when he came home to supper after the visit to the Bluebird.

"My! My!" exclaimed the lumber merchant, as he stopped in the hall to hang up his hat. "What a lot of talk all at once! Let me see--whose question shall I answer first?"

"Did you manage to get that poor boy a ride?" asked Mrs. Bobbsey.

It was the first time she had had a chance to ask her question.

"Answer mamma first," said Bert politely. "The rest of us can wait."

Mr. Bobbsey gave his older son a pleased look, and then replied:

"Yes, I found that one of our lumber wagons was going within half a mile of the village of Lemby, so I let the boy ride with the driver. It will give him a good lift."

"Indeed it will," said Mrs. Bobbsey. "I felt so sorry for him. I wish I could help him!"

"I hope the horses don't run away," spoke Freddie with such a serious air that they all laughed.

"I guess they won't run away, little fat fireman!" said Mr. Bobbsey, as he caught Freddie up in his arms. "They are good, steady horses, and they had a pretty heavy load to drag. So Will won't be in any danger. But I hope supper is ready. I'm hungry!"

"But you didn't answer my question," said Nan. "When are we going in the houseboat, father?"

"Oh, whenever school ends and your mother is ready," was the answer. "I should say in about two weeks."

"Good!" cried Bert. "And are we going to take Snap along?" he asked, as he caught sight of the trick dog outside, standing on his hind legs, while Sam Johnson held up a bone for him. Snap was "begging" for his supper, as he often did.

"Yes, I think we can find room for Snap on board," the lumber man said.

"What about our cat, Snoop?" asked Flossie. "I want to take Snoop along. Wouldn't you like to go in a boat, Snoop?" and Flossie picked the fat cat up in her arms. Snoop was quite an armful now. "Don't you want to go, Snoop?"

"Meow!" was all Snoop said, and that might have meant anything at all.

"Supper first," suggested Mr. Bobbsey, "and after that we'll talk about the boat."

The meal was a merry one, and there was much talk and laughter. As Dinah brought on one good thing to eat after another, Mrs. Bobbsey said:

"I hope every one has as nice a supper as we have."

"Were you thinking of any one in particular?" asked her husband.

"Yes, of that poor boy who came on the boat to-day," she answered. "I wonder if he has a good supper after his long walk this morning?"

"Well, they say Mr. Hardee doesn't feed his help any too well," spoke Mr. Bobbsey. "But now let's talk about our houseboat trip."

"Oh, what fun we'll have!" cried Freddie and Flossie, clapping their chubby hands.

"Did you plan a trip?" Mrs. Bobbsey wanted to know.

"Well, partly, yes. I thought we could go down Lake Metoka to Lemby Creek. We haven't been down that direction in some time."

"Lemby Creek!" exclaimed Bert. "Isn't that the name of the place where that boy came from?" "Well, Lemby is a town on Lemby Creek," spoke his father. "Will Watson works on Mr. Hardee's farm, and that is just outside the village. Lemby Creek is about ten miles long, and by going along that we can get into Lake Romano. That is a large body of water, and there is a waterfall at the farther end."

"A waterfall!" cried Freddie. "Oh, goodie! Can we go see it, papa?"

"I guess so," said Mr. Bobbsey. "We'll make this a long trip. It will take over a month, but of course we won't travel every day. Some days we'll just anchor the boat in a shady place, and---"

"Fish!" interrupted Bert.

"Yes, fish, or go in swimming--anything to have a good time," Mr. Bobbsey said.

"Oh, won't we have fun!" cried Freddie again. "We'll take Snoop and Snap along, and they'll like it, too."

"I guess Snap will, because he's fond of the water," said Bert, with a laugh. "But Snoop doesn't care for it."

"Snoop can sleep on deck in the sun," said Nan. "She'll like that. I wish I could ask one of my girl friends to come along with us for the houseboat trip. We have so many nice rooms on the Bluebird it seems a pity not to use them."

"And I'd like one of my boy chums, too," spoke Bert. Flossie and Freddie were busy trying to make Snoop do one of the tricks the circus lady had taught her. But Snoop wanted to go out in the kitchen, and have Dinah give her some supper.

"Company, eh?" exclaimed Mr. Bobbsey, slowly. "Well, I don't know. We have plenty of room on the Bluebird. I wonder how it would do to ask Harry and Dorothy to come with us?" he inquired of his wife.

"Oh, Cousin Harry!" cried Bert. "That would be fine!"

"And Cousin Dorothy!" added Nan. "She and I could have lovely times together. Do ask her, mother!"

"We might ask the cousins," agreed Mrs. Bobbsey. "They haven't been to visit us in some time, and I think both Harry and Dorothy would enjoy the trip."

Harry and Dorothy, as I have told you, were cousins

of the Bobbseys. Harry lived at Meadow Brook, in the country, and Dorothy at Ocean Cliff, near the sea.

"I'll write to-morrow," said Mrs. Bobbsey, "and find out if they can go with us. Now have we anything else to settle about our trip?"

"What about something to eat?" asked Freddie, in such a funny, anxious voice, that all the others laughed.

"My goodness, little fat fireman!" exclaimed his father. "Here you have just finished your supper, and you are already hungry again."

"Oh, I'm not hungry now," explained Freddie, "but I will be on the boat."

"Don't worry," said his mother. "Dinah is coming with us."

"Oh, then it will be all right," went on the little twin, with a contented sigh. "Come on, Flossie," he called to his small sister, "I know how we can have some fun. 'Scuse me," he murmured, as he and the other little twin slipped from their chairs.

Mr. and Mrs. Bobbsey, with Nan and Bert, remained at the table for some time longer, talking about the coming trip in the Bluebird. As Mr. Bobbsey had said, it would be about two weeks, yet, before they could start. There were two weeks more of school, but the classes would close earlier than usual that summer, because an addition was to be built to the school building, and the men wanted to get to work on it, to have it finished in time for school early in September.

"So we'll get an extra week or so of vacation," explained Bert. "And we'll spend it all on the houseboat."

"Well, perhaps not all of it," said Mr. Bobbsey. "I may not be able to stay with you all that while. But we'll spend a month or two on the Bluebird."

"What will we do the rest of vacation?" asked Bert.

"Oh, perhaps we'll go to the mountains, or some place like that," his mother said with a smile. "It isn't settled yet."

"Is it a high waterfall at Lake Romano?" asked Nan. "I just love them."

"Yes, it's a pretty high one," her father said. "I haven't been to Lake Romano in some years, but I remember it as a very beautiful place."

"I'm sure we shall enjoy it," Mrs. Bobbsey said.

"Is the fishing good?" Bert wanted to know.

"So I have heard. We'll take some poles and lines along, anyhow, and try our luck," his father replied.

Mr. Bobbsey pushed back his chair from the table, and looked around for the evening paper. Bert and Nan had some home work to do, to get ready their lessons for the next day's school classes, and Mrs. Bobbsey got out her sewing basket. There were always stockings to mend, if there was nothing else of the children's that needed attention.

The house was quiet except for the distant rattling of dishes in the kitchen, where fat Dinah was singing away as she worked. Suddenly her song ceased, and she was heard to exclaim:

"Now yo' want t' be careful, honey lamb! Doan't yo' go to muxin' up Dinah's clean kitchen flo'."

"No, we won't, Dinah!" replied Freddie's voice.

"If any gets spilled, I'll wipe it up," said Flossie.

"I wonder what those children are up to now?" remarked Mrs. Bobbsey, as she rolled up two stockings she had just darned.

"Oh, I guess they're all right," said Mr. Bobbsey easily, as he turned over a page of the evening paper.

The next moment there came a shout from Dinah in the kitchen.

"Stop it, Freddie. Stop it, I say!" cried the fat, colored cook. "Yo' suah am gittin' me all wet! Oh, there it goes ag'in! Stop it!"

"I--I can't!" cried Freddie. "Hold your hand over it, Flossie!"

"Oh, now it's squirting on me!" came in Flossie's tones. "Make it stop, Freddie."

"It--it won't stop!" was the frightened answer.

"Oh! Land ob massy!" shouted Dinah. "Sam! Sam! Mr. Bobbsey, come heah quick! It's squirtin' all ober!"

"Oh! Something has happened!" exclaimed Mrs. Bobbsey, starting toward the kitchen.

"Maybe a water pipe has burst," suggested Mr. Bobbsey, dropping his paper and making a jump toward the kitchen. As he did so, he heard Dinah cry again:

"Oh, yo' am all wet, honey lamb! Yo' is all soakin' wet! Oh, now it's comin' fo' me ag'in! Oh, stop it, Freddie! Stop it!"

"I--I can't!" was all Freddie said.

The next moment Mr. Bobbsey, followed by his wife, had reached the kitchen. There they saw a queer sight.

In the middle of the floor stood Flossie and

Freddie, water dripping from their hands and faces. Dinah, too, was wet, and she was fairly flying around, with a plate in one hand and a dish towel in the other.

And, all about the kitchen was spurting a stream of water, while over by the stove stood Freddie's toy fire engine. It was this engine that was spraying the water all over the room.

Chapter VII

The Two Cousins

"Oh, Freddie! What has happened?" cried Mrs. Bobbsey.

"It--it's the---" began Freddie, but that was as far as he got, for just then the stream of water from his toy engine spurted right into his open mouth.

"Shut it off!" cried Mr. Bobbsey. "Here, I'll do it!"

He started across the kitchen floor.

"Look out, Massa Bobbsey!" yelled Dinah. "It'll cotch yo' shuah. It done cotched me!" and then as she saw the little rubber hose of Freddie's fire engine swing around, and the nozzle point at her, the fat cook ran into the dish-closet and shut the door.

"How did it happen?" asked Mrs. Bobbsey, not so excited, now that she found nothing serious was the matter.

"Freddie--Freddie--he wanted to try how his fire engine worked, 'cause he hadn't played with it this week," explained Flossie. Freddie was busy wiping the water from his face. "So he filled the tank, and wound it up, and now--and now--it won't--it won't stop-squirtin'!" went on Flossie. "It--it---"

And then she, too, had to stop talking, for the hose was spurting water at her now.

"I'll shut it off. Something must be the matter with the spring," said Mr. Bobbsey. He walked toward Freddie's fire engine, which was pretty large, for a toy. But before he reached it, the water hose had swung around, and, instead of sprinkling Flossie, was aimed at Mr. Bobbsey. However he did not mind. Holding the newspaper in front of his face, Freddie's father reached the fire engine, and turned off the machinery that pumped the water.

"There!" he cried. "The fire's out! The only damage is from water," and he laughed, for he was wet, and so were Mrs. Bobbsey, Flossie and Freddie; and the kitchen itself was pretty well sprinkled.

"What's it all about?" asked Bert, for he and Nan, who had been studying their lessons, had heard the noise of the excitement, and had run to the kitchen to see what had caused it.

"Oh, Freddie turned in a false alarm," said Mr. Bobbsey. "How did you come to put water in your engine, when mamma has told you not to do so in the house?" he asked the little boy.

"Be--be--cause," said Freddie slowly, "I wanted to see if it would-- work. I'm going to take it on the houseboat with me."

"Well, I guess it worked all right," Bert said, as he looked around at the wet kitchen. Luckily there was oil cloth on the floor, and the walls were painted, so the water really did no harm.

Dinah slowly opened the door of the dish-closet, and peered out.

"Am it all done, honey lamb?" she asked, looking at Freddie.

"Yes, Dinah! It's all done squirtin'," he said. "I guess there isn't any more water, anyhow."

"No," said Mr. Bobbsey, with a smile, as he looked in the tank of the engine, "it's all pumped out."

Freddie's toy fire engine was a large and expensive one his uncle had given him on Christmas. It was made as nearly like a real engine as possible, only instead of working by steam, it worked by a spring. When a spring was wound up, it operated a small pump in the engine. The pump made water spurt out through a little rubber hose, and the water for the engine was poured into a tank. The tank held about two gallons, so you see when it was all pumped out in the kitchen, and spurted on those in the room, it made them pretty wet.

"It's clean water," said Nan, when every one had somewhat cooled down, "and it's so warm to-night, I wouldn't mind being sprayed with a hose myself."

"Still, Freddie shouldn't have done it," said Mrs. Bobbsey. "I have told you not to play with your engine in the house, when it had water in it, Freddie. How did you come to disobey me?" she asked, for usually the little fellow was very good about minding.

"I--I didn't mean to, mamma," he said "First I just wanted to see if the engine tank leaked, so I put in some water. I didn't think it would hurt, out here on the kitchen oil cloth, and honestly I wasn't going to squirt it."

"No, I suppose not," said Mr. Bobbsey, wiping the water from his face, and glancing at his soaked newspaper.

"So I just filled the tank with water from the sink," explained Freddie.

"I--I helped him," confessed Flossie, ready to take her share of the blame.

"What happened next?" asked Mrs. Bobbsey.

"Why--er--I just wanted to see if the spring was all right, so I wound that up," Freddie went on. "Then I sort of forgot about the water in the tank, and before I knew it, why it--it went off--sudden like."

"Land ob massy! I should say it done did go off--suddint laik!" exclaimed Dinah. "Fust I knowed I was dryin' de dishes an' den I got a mouth full ob watah. I shuah did t'ink a watah pipe had done gone an' busted. I shuah did!"

"It--it just kept on squirtin'!" said Freddie. "I couldn't stop it like it always used to stop."

"No, the pump is out of order," said Mr. Bobbsey, as he looked at the now empty fire engine. "It wouldn't stop pumping. Well, I'm glad it wasn't a real fire, and glad that no one is hurt. Put your engine away now, Freddie, and, after this, don't play with water in the house, when mamma has told you not to."

"I won't," promised Freddie. "But it's a good engine, isn't it?"

"Oh, yes, it's a good engine, all right."

"And I can take it on the houseboat, can't I?"

"Yes, but you won't need to put any water in. There'll be enough in the creek and lakes," said Mrs. Bobbsey with a smile. "Come now, Flossie and Freddie, you are wet, so you might as well get undressed and go to bed. It is nearly time, anyhow, and you have had quite a day of it. Off to bed!"

Off to bed the twins went.

Dinah wiped up the kitchen, and, as she did so, she murmured over and over again: "It shuah did go off suddint laik! It shuah did!"

Flossie and Freddie, little the worse for their wetting, went off to school next day, with Nan and Bert. The two sets of twins talked of many things on their way to their classes, but, most of all, they talked of the coming trip on the houseboat, and of the accident to the fire engine the night before.

"I do hope Cousin Dorothy can come with us," said Nan, as she left Bert to walk along with Nellie Parks.

"And I hope Harry can go," said Bert. "Better hurry along, Freddie," he called to his little brother. "There goes your bell, and yours, too, Flossie."

The two little tots turned into the gate of the school that led to the yard where the smallest pupils formed in line.

"Well, even if Harry and Dorothy can't go, I'll take my fire engine," said Freddie.

"And we'll take Snoop and Snap, so we won't be lonesome," suggested Flossie. "Oh, won't it be fun, Freddie!"

"Yes, I wish it was time to go now. I'm tired of school," said the little fellow.

But school must go on, whether there are houseboat parties or not, so the Bobbsey twins had to study their lessons. I think that day, however, Bert must have been thinking of other things than his books, for when the teacher asked him what an island was, Bert gave a queer answer. Instead of saying it was a body of land, surrounded by water, Bert said:

"An island is a fire engine in the kitchen."

"Why, Bert Bobbsey! What are you thinking of?" asked the teacher.

"Oh, I--I was thinking of something that happened at our house last night," Bert went on, while all the children in the room laughed.

"Then you'd better tell us about it," suggested Miss Teeter, the instructor, for she was very kind. So Bert told of Freddie's mishap, and how it was he happened to be thinking of that instead of the right answer to the question about the island.

"I hear you have a houseboat, Bert," said John Blake, a boy in the same room, as the children came out of school that afternoon.

"Yes, my father bought the one Mr. Marvin owned," said Bert. "It's a fine one, too. We're going to have a trip in her soon."

"You're a lucky boy!" exclaimed John. "Can't you take me down and show me over the boat?"

"I'd like to," said Bert, "but father said I wasn't to go aboard, when he was not with me."

"Pooh! He'll never know," suggested Danny Rugg, a boy with whom Bert had had more or less trouble. "You needn't tell your father you went to the boat. Come on, take us down and let's see it."

"No," said Bert, quietly but firmly. "Maybe my father wouldn't know I had been on board, but I'd know it."

"Aw, you're a fraid-cat!" sneered Danny. "Come on, take us down, and we'll have some fun."

"No," said Bert with a shake of his head. "I'm sorry.

Some other time, after I've asked my father if I may, I'll show you all over the Bluebird."

"I want to go now," Danny said.

"Oh, there's plenty of time," spoke John, pleasantly. "I wouldn't want Bert to do what his father told him not to, just to oblige me. I'll see the boat some other time, Bert; that will do just as well."

"Huh! He's a fraid-cat!" muttered Danny again, as he shuffled off, muttering to himself. Several times he had made trouble for the Bobbsey twins, and Bert was not any too friendly with him. Danny was a bully in the school.

Bert wished, very much indeed, that he could have taken some of his boy friends down to the houseboat, but his father had a good reason for not wanting any boys aboard, unless he could be with them. Workmen were making certain changes in the craft, and doing some painting inside and outside.

A few days after this, when the Bobbsey twins reached home from school, Mrs. Bobbsey met them at the door, saying:

"I have good news for you, children!"

"What is it?" cried Bert.

"Don't we have to go to school any more?" Freddie.

"Are we going on the houseboat sooner than we expected?" Nan wanted to know.

"It's about your two cousins--Harry and Dorothy," went on Mrs. Bobbsey. "They have both accepted our invitations, and they will come with us on the trip! Won't that be nice?"

"Lovely!" exclaimed Nan, her eyes shining with delight. "Dorothy and I'll have such nice times together!"

"And Harry and I'll catch a lot of fish," declared Bert.

The days went on. The houseboat was nearly ready for her trip. Very soon school would close.

"Come on, Bert, can't you show us over the boat now?" asked Danny Rugg one afternoon, on his way home from school, with Nan's brother, and some other boys.

"I can't to-day, but perhaps I can to-morrow," said Bert. "I'll ask my father."

"He'll never know about it," tempted Danny again, but Bert could not be influenced that way.

"Never mind, I'll fix you!" threatened Danny, which was what he usually said, when he could not have his own way.

Bert thought little of the threat at the time, though later he recalled it vividly.

It was that night, just as the smaller twins were getting ready for bed, that the telephone in the Bobbsey house rang out a call.

"I'll answer it," said Mr. Bobbsey, as he went to the instrument. "Hello!" he called. Then his wife and children heard him cry:

"What! Is that so! That's too bad! Yes, I'll attend to it right away. I wonder how it happened?"

"Oh, what has happened?" cried Mrs. Bobbsey, in alarm.

"Is the lumber yard on fire again?" asked Freddie, thinking of his toy engine.

"Not as bad as that," said Mr. Bobbsey, as he quickly put on his hat. "But the watchman at the dock just telephoned me that our houseboat, the Bluebird, has gotten adrift, and is floating out into the lake."

Chapter VIII

Off in the "Bluebird"

For a few seconds after Mr. Bobbsey told of the news
he had heard over the telephone, none of the twins
seemed to know what to say. They just stared at their
father, and I really believe, for a moment, that Flossie
and Freddie thought he was playing a joke on them.
Then Mrs. Bobbsey seemed to understand it.

"What!" she cried. "Our houseboat adrift?"

"That's what the watchman tells me," said Mr.
Bobbsey, as he started for the front door.

"But who did it?" asked Bert, managing to get his
tongue in working order.

"Can't you get her back again?" asked Nan. "Our
boat, I mean."

"Let me come with you!" pleaded Freddie.

"And I want to come, too!" added Flossie. She
seldom wanted to be left behind, when her twin brother
went anywhere.

"No, no! You children must stay here," said Mr.
Bobbsey. "I will hurry down to the lake, and come right
back. I'll tell you all about it, when I return."

"But what could have happened?" asked Mrs. Bobbsey. "What would make our boat go adrift?"

"Oh, some of the ropes might have come loose," replied her husband. "Or the ropes might even have been cut through, rubbing against the dock. The wind is blowing a little, and that is sending the boat out into the lake. I'll get one of our steam tugs, and go after her. It will not take long nor be hard work to bring her back."

A number of small steam tugs were owned by Mr. Bobbsey for use in hauling lumber boats, and lumber rafts about Lake Metoka. Some of these tugs were always at the dock, and one always had steam up, ready for instant use.

"Well, I hope you get the Bluebird back all right," said Bert. "We don't want to miss our trip, especially after we have asked Harry and Dorothy."

"Oh, it would be too bad to disappoint them," put in Nan.

"Oh, I'll get the boat back all right," declared Mr. Bobbsey.

Flossie and Freddie breathed sighs of relief. They were not worried now, for they knew their father would do as he said.

Fat Dinah put her head in through the door of the sitting room.

"Am anyt'ing de mattah?" she asked. "I done heah yo' all talkin' in heah, an' I t'inks maybe dat honey lamb Freddie done got his steam enjine squirtin' watah ag'in."

"Not this time, Dinah," said Mrs. Bobbsey, for the

cook was almost like one of the family. Then the twins' mother explained what the trouble was.

"I 'clar t' goodness!" Dinah exclaimed. "Suffin's always happenin' in dish yeah fambily."

It was not a very serious happening this time. Mr. Bobbsey hurried down to his lumber yard in the darkness of the June evening.

He was gone about an hour, when the telephone rang. On account of the little excitement Flossie and Freddie had been allowed to stay up, although it was long past their usual bedtime.

"I'll answer it," said Mrs. Bobbsey, as the telephoned bell stopped jingling, for Bert had started from his seat.

"Oh, it's papa," the twins' mother went on, after she had listened for a second after saying "Hello!"

"Is the boat all right?" asked Nan, anxiously.

"Yes," answered her mother, and then she turned to listen to the rest of Mr. Bobbsey's talk over the telephone.

"Papa went after the Bluebird, and brought her safely back," Mrs. Bobbsey explained, when she had hung up the receiver. "He'll be here in a few minutes to tell us all about it. He telephoned from the lumber office after he had our boat safe."

"Oh, I'm so glad the boat's all right," said Nan.

"Pooh, I knowed it would be--when papa went after it," said Freddie, with a sleepy yawn.

"You must say 'knew,' not 'knowed,' dear," spoke Mamma Bobbsey. "And now I think it is time for you and Flossie to go to bed."

Neither of the smaller twins offered any objection. They were too sleepy to want to stay up and listen to the story of the bringing back of the Bluebird.

Nan and Bert were anxious to hear it, and Mr. Bobbsey came in soon after Flossie and Freddie were tucked in bed. He told the story of the drifting houseboat.

"How did it break loose?" asked Bert.

"It didn't break loose," said his father. "Some one untied the knots in the ropes."

"Untied!" cried Mrs. Bobbsey. "How did it happen?"

"Why, some one went aboard the boat," explained Mr. Bobbsey, "and I think it must have been some boys, for I found this cap," and he held up a gray one.

"Why!" cried Bert when he saw it. "That's Danny Rugg's cap!"

"I thought so," went on Mr. Bobbsey. "Danny, and some of his chums, must have gone on the boat early this evening. They played about, as boys will, and some of them, either on purpose or accidentally, must have loosed the knots in the ropes before coming ashore. Then the boat just drifted away after that."

"Those boys had no right to go on our boat!" said Nan.

"No, they had not," agreed her father, "But I'm glad there was no real damage done. The watchman saw the Bluebird soon after she had drifted away from the dock, and he telephoned me. I went out in one of our tugs and soon brought her back. So you think this is Danny Rugg's cap, Bert?"

"I'm sure of it, yes, sir. Danny wanted me to take him, and some of the other boys, on the boat, but I wouldn't."

"I'm glad you remembered what I told you," spoke Mr. Bobbsey, and Bert blushed with pleasure.

"I'll give Danny his cap in the morning," Bert went on. "It may surprise him to know where he lost it."

"I don't believe you can surprise that Danny Rugg very much," said Mrs. Bobbsey.

The next morning, when Bert took Danny's cap to school with him, and handed it to the boy who had caused so much trouble, a queer look came over Danny's face.

"Thanks," he said. "I was wondering where I left that. I guess I must have dropped it, when I was-- playing football over in the fields."

"No, you dropped it on our houseboat, the Bluebird, just before you and the other fellows untied the ropes that let her go adrift," said Bert. "And you'd better keep off her after this!"

"Huh! I'm not afraid of your father!" was all Danny growled, as he stuffed his cap in his pocket, for he had worn another to school.

When Danny's chums learned that it was known who had set the boat adrift, they were rather frightened. When they realized the damage they might have done, they kept away from Mr. Bobbsey's lumber yard for a long time.

One day, about a week after this, the Bobbsey twins hurried home from school without stopping to play with any of their friends.

"Why are you in such a hurry?" asked Grace Lavine of Nan.

"We expect our cousins to-day," Nan answered. "Then we are going to get ready to go away in our houseboat."

Surely enough, when the twins reached home, there the cousins were to greet them--Dorothy and Harry, one from the seashore, and the other from the country.

"Oh, but I'm so glad to see you!" cried Nan, as she hugged and kissed Dorothy.

"And I'm so glad to come," Dorothy answered with a smile. "It was lovely of you to invite me to go on your boat."

"We'll have a lot of fun," said Bert to Harry.

"That's what we will," replied the boy from the country.

"We're both awful glad to see you!" chimed in Flossie, speaking both for herself and for Freddie. "But we can't play with the fire engine."

"Not if we put water in," added Freddie.

"What in the world do they mean?" asked Dorothy, wonderingly.

"Oh, I'll have to tell you," laughed Nan, as she explained about the accident.

The cousins had much to tell the twins, and talk about, and the twins had as much more to tell, so, for a time, there was a merry sound of talk and laughter.

Dorothy and Harry had come by different trains, one from the seashore and the other from the country, but they had reached the Bobbsey house at the same time. Their schools had not yet closed, but as they were both well advanced in their studies, their parents had allowed them to leave their classes ahead of time, since they were both sure to "pass."

"Just think!" cried Nan, when there was a moment of quiet. "In three days more our school will close, and then we'll go on the trip."

"Won't it be lovely!" murmured Dorothy.

I leave you to imagine all that took place in those three days. Schooldays came to an end, and the Bobbsey twins were among those at the heads of their classes. Then came a packing-up time, and the Bobbsey house was a scene of great excitement. Trunks and boxes were taken aboard the Bluebird, a man was hired to run the gasoline engine. Plenty of good things to eat were stowed away in the kitchen lockers, as cupboards are called on a boat. At last all was ready for the start.

Snoop and Snap, of course, were on hand, as was Dinah. Mr. Bobbsey saw to it that his family, and the two cousins, were safely aboard, and then he gave the order to cast off the lines. The Bluebird floated away from the dock, and out into the lake that was almost as blue as her name.

"All aboard!" cried Bert.

"Toot! Toot!" whistled Freddie, pretending to be an engine.

"Oh, look out! You're stepping on my doll!" screamed Flossie, who had put her toy down on the deck a moment.

"Good-bye! Good-bye!" called Nan to Grace

Lavine, and some others of her girl friends, who had come down to the dock to see them off. "Good-bye!"

"Good-bye!" echoed the girls, waving their hands.

"Come on!" called Bert to Harry, as he started for the lower cabin.

"What are you going to do?" asked the boy from the country.

"Let's get out our fishing poles. Maybe we can catch something for dinner."

"That's right!" agreed Harry.

Slowly the Bluebird moved out into the lake, for the gasoline engine was working. The houseboat trip of the Bobbsey twins had begun, and many things were to happen before it was to end.

Chapter IX

Snoop and Snap

Nan and Dorothy, after waving good-bye to the girl friends on the dock, went down to the living room of the houseboat. There they found Mrs. Bobbsey and Dinah putting away some of the things that had been brought on board at the last moment.

"I 'clar t' goodness!" exclaimed the colored cook, "dish yeah houseboatin' am wuss dan movin'!"

"Oh, not quite as bad as that," said Mrs. Bobbsey, with a laugh. "But what are you going to do, Nan, dear? Do you like it, Dorothy?"

"Oh! indeed I do," answered the "seashore cousin," as Nan called her to distinguish her from Harry, who lived in the country.

"We are just going to our rooms for a minute, mother," Nan answered. "I want to show Dorothy my new sailor suit."

Every body on the houseboat was busy, even down to Flossie and Freddie, and the two little twins were busy having fun.

Mrs. Bobbsey and Dinah were engaged in putting to rights the different rooms, for there were a number on the Bluebird, which was built for a large family. Bert and Harry were up on deck fishing, as the boat moved slowly through the blue waters of Metoka Lake. Flossie and Freddie, as I have said, were playing, the little girl with her doll, and Freddie with a new toy his father had bought him.

As for Mr. Bobbsey, he was down in the engine room with "Captain White." Mr. White was one of Mr. Bobbsey's men who had once been in charge of a tugboat, but one day there was an accident aboard, and Mr. White was made lame for life.

But Mr. Bobbsey liked his faithful employee, and kept him at work, and since Mr. White could not do heavy tasks, he was allowed to do easy ones.

Mr. White was called "Captain" by every one, though he was not really a captain. Still, he knew a great deal about boats, the weather clouds and storms, and all things such as sea captains are supposed to know.

When Mr. Bobbsey bought Mr. Marvin's houseboat, he at once began to think of some one who could sail it for him, and take care of the gasoline engine. Naturally, he thought of Captain White. So the Bluebird was put in charge of Captain White, who, you may be sure, was very glad to be on the water again, even if it was only in a slow- moving houseboat, and not in a swift steam tug.

Mr. Bobbsey and Captain White were down in the motor, or engine room together. Mr. Bobbsey was learning how to run the gasoline engine.

I have told you how the Bluebird was driven along through the water by a small engine. It was not a steam engine, such as are found in many boats, but a gasoline one, such as those in most automobiles.

Mr. Bobbsey did not intend to sail very fast in the houseboat. In fact, for many days, he expected to just drift along, or push the boat with a long pole through some shallow creek, or in parts of the lake where it was not deep. When he wanted to move more quickly from place to place, there was the gasoline engine all ready to use. And Captain White knew how to use it.

Mr. Bobbsey came up out of the little motor room after a while, and watched his wife and Dinah putting things away. The boat was moving down the lake.

"Oh, look at your face!" suddenly cried Mrs. Bobbsey.

"What's the matter with it?" asked her husband, putting his hand up to his nose, as almost any person will do when you speak of his face.

"It's all black!" went on Mrs. Bobbsey. "So are your hands. Oh, Richard! What have you been doing?"

"Learning to run the gasoline engine," he said. "I want to know how it works so that if we need to start any time when Captain White is on shore, or asleep, I can do it."

"I hope you won't start off any time when Captain White is on shore," said Mrs. Bobbsey. "You don't know enough about a boat to run it without him."

"Very well, then. I promise I'll run the gasoline engine only when Captain White is asleep," said Mr. Bobbsey, with a laugh. "And then, if anything happens, I'll only have to awaken him, and ask him what is wrong."

"That's the best plan," said Mrs. Bobbsey, also laughing. "And now you had better go wash your face. Some one might see you--looking like that."

There was a nice little bathroom aboard the Bluebird, and Mr. Bobbsey was soon splashing away with the water and soap. Meanwhile Mrs. Bobbsey and Dinah finished their work, and went up on deck.

It was a very pleasant day, and with the sun shining down from a blue sky overhead, just warm enough, and not too hot, with a gentle breeze that hardly ruffled the surface of the lake, but which made it delightfully cool as the boat moved slowly along. In short, it was just perfect weather, as the Bobbsey twins started off on their houseboat.

Nan and Dorothy, having finished looking at each other's dresses, which always seems to delight girls, had come up on deck so that now the whole Bobbsey family, and their country, and seashore cousin visitors also, were there.

"Have you caught any fish yet?" asked Mr. Bobbsey, walking over to where Bert and Harry were dangling their lines in the water.

"Not yet, but we've had two or three bites," said Bert, hopefully.

"I think you'll have better luck when we reach some quiet place, and anchor," Mr. Bobbsey went on. "At any rate, you need not worry, if you don't catch any fish. Dinah will be able to give us something else for dinner, I think."

"I think so, too," said Harry with a laugh. "I can smell something cooking now."

This was so. For, though the Bobbseys had started early that morning, there was so much to do that it was now nearly noon. To them it seemed only an hour or so since they had started. Dinah was a good cook. She kept one eye on the clock and the other on the things she was cooking. And she made up her mind that the meals would be on time, even if they were served on a houseboat. So it was the cooking of dinner that Harry smelled.

"Oh, Dorothy!" exclaimed Nan, after a little while, during which the two girls looked across the lake to the distant shores they had left. "I must show you a new trick Snap has learned."

"What! Another trick?" cried Dorothy. "My! He knows a lot of them now. He certainly is a clever dog!"

Snap, as I have told you, used to belong to a circus before the Bobbseys bought him, so perhaps learning tricks came easier to him than to most dogs.

"Yes, I taught him this trick myself," went on Nan. "He will walk around on his hind legs, and carry a doll in his front paws, just like a nurse girl. When I dress him up in one of my old skirts and a jacket, he is too funny for anything! I'll make him do the trick now, only I won't dress him up, for I can't find the clothes he wears. I don't believe we brought them. But I'll make him carry the doll for you. Here, Snap!" called Nan.

The dog, who had been sleeping in a sunny Spot on deck, near Snoop, the black cat, sprang up, when he heard his name called.

"Where are you going to get a doll for him to carry?" asked Dorothy.

"I'll take Flossie's. You'll let sister take your doll to make Snap do a trick, won't you, dear?" she asked.

"Yes, Nan," answered flaxen-haired Flossie. "I just love to see Snap do that trick! He carries the doll so cute!"

Flossie brought her doll to Nan, and Snap stood near, wagging his tail, for he seemed to know what was coming.

"Now, Snap," said Nan, pointing her finger at the dog, "I want you to show Dorothy how you play nurse-girl, and carry a doll."

"Bow wow!" barked Snap. That was what he always said when any one spoke to him. I suppose he knew what he meant, but no one else did. At any rate, he seemed to understand what was said to him.

"Up, Snap! Up!" called Nan suddenly, and Snap rose on his hind legs, holding his fore paws out in front of him, so Nan could place the doll on them.

This the little girl did, putting Flossie's "sawdust baby" carefully across Snap's paws.

"Now take the doll for a walk!" ordered Nan, and, with another bark, off Snap started, parading across the deck.

"Oh, isn't he too cute!" cried Dorothy, laughing and clapping her hands. "Oh, what a smart dog he is!"

"Isn't he!" agreed Nan. "Bert said I never could teach him to do a trick, but I did."

"Indeed you did!" agreed Dorothy.

"Now come back here, Snap!" ordered Nan. But just then something happened.

How it was no one knew exactly, but Bert suddenly

caught a fish. He was so surprised at getting a hard bite on his line, that he jerked it up quickly. Something flashed in the sunlight, and, the next moment, a little sunfish landed flapping on the deck, right in front of the sleeping black cat Snoop.

"Flop!" went the fish, and Snoop awakened with a jump. Up to her feet she leaped like a flash, and then she saw the fish. Snoop was very fond of fish, and made a spring for the one Bert had caught. But the fish was wet and slippery, and no sooner had Snoop pounced on it with her claws than the fish slid across the deck of the houseboat. Snoop slid after it, just as she often slid across the kitchen oilcloth, when she sprang for a piece of string that Flossie or Freddie would pull along to make the cat play.

Right across the deck, after the slippery fish slid Snoop, and, the next instant, the poor cat had slid right off the deck, and fallen into the lake with a splash!

Chapter X

Down the Creek

"There goes Snoop!"

"Oh, somebody get her!"

Nan and Dorothy both shouted at the same time. As for Bert, he was so surprised at having caught a fish, and at seeing the cat slide off the deck with it, that he could say nothing. It was almost the same with Harry. He had jumped to his feet, however, and had run toward Snoop, but too late.

Then, all of a sudden, Snap, with a loud bark, gave one spring, and the next moment he had jumped right over the deck railing, under which Snoop had slid. Right over it went Snap, and down into the lake. For he knew that Snoop had fallen in, and, being the kind of a dog that asks nothing better than to save something, or somebody, from the water, Snap was right on hand.

"Oh, my doll! My doll!" cried Flossie. "Snap is taking my doll into the lake with him! Come back, Snap! Come back!"

Snap did not stop to listen. He had, indeed, taken Flossie's doll with him. He had been holding it on his front paws as Snoop slid overboard, and, as he gave a jump, Snap did not come down on all four legs. He jumped while he was yet standing on his hind ones, and of course the doll went over the rail with him.

"What has happened?" cried Mrs. Bobbsey, as she heard the screaming, and the splashes in the water. "Have any of the children fallen in?" For she had gone to another part of the deck, with Dinah, out of sight of the twins for a moment. Now she came hurrying back, and a single look showed her that the children were all safe.

"What has happened?" she asked again.

"As nearly as I can figure out," said Mr. Bobbsey, "Bert caught a fish, Snoop tried to get it and fell into the water, and now Snap has gone in after Snoop."

"And Snap has my doll! She'll get all wet--she'll be drowned!" cried Flossie.

"I'll get her for you," offered Harry. But just now they were all anxious to see what Snap and Snoop did. Mr. and Mrs. Bobbsey and the children looked over the side of the houseboat. They saw the black cat swimming about in the lake, and Snap, who was a fine water-dog, was paddling toward her.

"Hadn't you better stop the boat?" asked Mrs. Bobbsey, for the Bluebird was slowly floating away from the dog and the cat.

"Yes, I guess it would be best," said Mr. Bobbsey. So he called out:

"Captain! Captain White! Stop the boat! Something overboard!"

Down in the little motor room Mr. White heard the shout, and he at once shut off the gasoline engine.

Then he came up on deck as fast as his lame leg would let him, to see what was wrong.

"What's that you say?" he asked. "Somebody fell overboard?"

"The dog and the cat," explained Mr. Bobbsey. "I wonder how we can get them out? It's Snoop and Snap who are in the water."

"And my doll!" added Flossie. "I want my doll back!"

"Oh, yes, and Flossie's doll," added Mr. Bobbsey. "I guess you'd better get in the rowboat, Captain White. It will be easier to lift them out from there."

"I'll do it, Mr. Bobbsey," the captain said, as he limped down stairs again. By this time Snap had swum to where poor Snoop was paddling about in the water. The dog gently took hold of the cat by the back of the neck, where her loose fur would give a good hold. Then Snap, holding Snoop's head well up out of the water, started back for the houseboat.

"Good old Snap!" called Mr. Bobbsey. Snap wanted to bark and wag his tail, as he always did when any one spoke pleasantly to him, but he knew if he opened his mouth to bark now, he would have to drop Snoop. And Snap had hard enough work swimming, without trying to wag his tail. On he came toward the boat.

By this time Captain White had gotten into the small boat, which was pulled after the Bluebird, by a rope, and he was rowing toward the dog. Seeing that the smaller boat was nearer, Snap swam toward that, instead of toward the larger one. He held Snoop carefully up out of the water.

"That's a good dog, Snap!" called Captain White, as Snap came nearer. "I'll take her now."

The engineer lifted poor, wet, dripping Snoop into his boat. She crawled close up to Captain White, for she was much frightened. After Snap had delivered the cat he had rescued, he turned back again.

"Where are you going?" asked Captain White. "Don't you want to get in my boat, too, Snap?"

"Bow wow!" barked Snap. This time he could open his mouth, as he was not carrying a cat.

"Oh, he's going to get my doll!" cried Flossie. "Look, Snap is after my doll!"

And so he was. After taking Snoop safely to the boat, Snap had seen Flossie's doll floating on the top of the water, and had swum toward that, just as he would have gone toward a floating stick, had there been one near.

"OK, now he's got her!" cried the happy Flossie. "Now Snap has my doll. Goodie!"

"And, as she's a wooden doll, the water won't hurt her," said Nan, with a laugh, "Everything is coming out all right."

And so it seemed.

Taking the doll in his mouth, as he had taken the cat, Snap swam back toward the small boat, where Captain White waited for him, now and then petting poor Snoop. Just as the dog had done with the cat, so he did with the doll, giving her to the engineer of the Bluebird. Then, seeing that his work was all done, Snap once more swam toward the big boat, not trying to get into the small one.

"Good dog, Snap!" cried Mr. Bobbsey, as he leaned over to lift him in, for there were no steps by which to climb up the side of the Bluebird.

This time Snap barked and wagged his tail, and then he gave himself a big shake to get rid of the water. He sent a regular shower of spray all about.

"Come, girls!" cried Mrs. Bobbsey with a laugh, "this is no place for us. We haven't our bathing suits on!" and she, with Nan and Dorothy, ran back out of the way of the scattering drops from Snap's shaggy coat.

A little later Captain White rowed up with Snoop and Flossie's doll, and the little girl at once said she was going to put a dry dress on the doll, so she wouldn't "take cold."

"Well," said Mr. Bobbsey, when the excitement had died down. "That's over, at any rate. All that over one little fish!"

"That's so--my fish started it all!" said Bert. "I wonder what became of it?" and he looked at his empty hook, dangling from the line of his pole.

"The fish dropped off," said Harry. "I saw it. But it was only a little one. It wouldn't have been any good."

"Poor Snoop!" said Mrs. Bobbsey. "All your trouble for nothing! You didn't get the fish."

"Oh, I'll soon catch some more for her, won't we, Harry?" Bert asked.

"That's what we will," answered the country cousin.

"Now if yo' folks am all done fallin' ovahbo'd I'se ready t' gib yo' all suffin t' eat," said Dinah, coming up from the dining-room.

"And I think we are ready to eat," said Mrs. Bobbsey. "This traveling on the water has given me an appetite."

"I guess it has all of us," spoke Mr. Bobbsey with a laugh, as he noticed the eager, hungry looks on the faces of the children.

"And give Snoop and Snap something good and hot, so they won't take cold," suggested Nan. "Though I don't believe they will this weather, it's so warm."

"I'm going to give my dollie hot chocolate," said Flossie, who, by this time, had put a dry dress on her pet.

The meal was a merry one, though at first the children, especially Flossie and Freddie, were too excited to eat. Then, too, it was so strange eating on a boat that was moving through the water, for the engine had been started again. Several times, during the meal, the two smaller twins jumped up from the table to run to the windows and look out over the lake. At last their mother said:

"Now, Flossie and Freddie, you must sit still and finish your dinner. Otherwise you may be ill. You'll have plenty of time to see things after you leave the table."

Snap was soon dry, from lying in the sun, and, a little later, Snoop was as warm and fluffy as before she had fallen into the lake. She picked out a warm spot on deck near Snap, for they had been the best of friends since the first day they had met, when Snoop came back from her long trip to Cuba, as I have told you in another book.

All the rest of that day the houseboat traveled over

Lake Metoka. The children sat on Heck, and watched other boats pass them. Some of them were loaded with lumber for Mr. Bobbsey. Others were pleasure boats, and those on board waved their hands to the Bobbsey twins and their cousins.

"Are we going to travel all night?" asked Bert of his father, when Dinah called that supper was ready.

"No, we are going to anchor soon. We will go a little nearer shore first, though."

"And when will we start through Lemby Creek toward Lake Romano?"

"Oh, in a day or so, I fancy."

It was such a pleasant evening, that even the little twins were allowed to stay up on deck past their usual bedtime, looking at the twinkling stars, and the lights of other boats on the lake.

When Flossie and Freddie did get to bed, they did not go to sleep at once. It was very strange to them, sleeping on a boat in the water.

Finally the two little people dozed off, and then the older folks went to bed. In the middle of the night Freddie woke up. At first he could not remember where he was, and he wondered at the queer rocking motion of the boat, for a little wind was ruffling the lake.

Suddenly there came a loud toot.

"Mamma! Papa! I heard something!" cried Freddie, sitting up.

"Yes, dear. It was only the whistle of another boat," said his mother, who was in the room next to him. "Go to sleep again."

Freddie did.

"Well, I sure am going to catch some fish to-day," said Bert, when he and Harry went up on deck next morning, after breakfast.

"We'll try, anyhow," Harry said. "We're nearer shore now, and the fishing ought to be better. I'll get my line.".

Whether it was on account of the bait they used, or because the fish were not plentiful, the boys did not know, but they did not get even one bite. Anyhow, they had fun.

The Bluebird went slowly across the lake. The Bobbseys were in no hurry, and they wanted to enjoy the pleasant weather. For three days they sailed over the blue waters, and then Mr. Bobbsey told Captain White to steer toward Lemby Creek.

"We'll go through the creek into Lake Romano," said the twins' father. "That is a much larger lake. We'll spend most of our houseboat vacation there. We will also visit the big waterfall."

"That will be lovely!" exclaimed Dorothy. Though she lived near the sea, she also loved inland waters, such as rivers and lakes.

The houseboat moved so slowly, and was such a safe craft, that Bert and Harry were allowed to steer at times, when Mr. Bobbsey or Captain White stood near them in case of any danger. The two boy cousins had taken turns steering, until the Bluebird was close to the place where Lemby Creek emptied into Lake Metoka.

"You'd better let me take the steering wheel, now," said Mr. Bobbsey to Bert. "There is a little current from the creek into the lake, and we don't want to run ashore."

In a little while the houseboat was safely in the creek. This stream of water was narrow, though it was deep enough to float the Bluebird easily. The shores were so close, at times, that the tree branches overhung the deck, and brushed the rails.

"I could almost jump ashore," said Harry.

"But you mustn't try it!" cautioned his aunt. "You might fall in, and Snap couldn't rescue you as easily as he did Snoop or the doll."

As the houseboat went slowly around a bend in the creek, Nan, who stood in front, near her father, suddenly uttered a cry, and pointed toward shore.

"What is it?" asked Mr. Bobbsey.

"There's that boy--Will Watson!" spoke Nan. "You know--the one who liked our boat so," and she pointed to the strange lad who worked for Mr. Hardee. The boy was walking along the shore of the creek, a fish pole over his shoulder.

"Oh, let's ask him how to catch fish!" proposed Bert. "We haven't had any luck at all!"

Chapter XI

The Mean Man

Certainly it seemed a good place to fish, in Lemby Creek, for there were many shady pools near the banks--pools that looked as though fish swam in them, just waiting to be caught.

As Harry and Bert looked more closely at the boy Nan had pointed out to them, they saw that he carried a string of fish, as well as the pole.

"Oh, he's caught some!" cried Bert. "Let's ask how he does it."

"And where he caught them," suggested Harry.

"I will," agreed Bert. "Hey there, Will!" he called. "Where'd you get the fish?"

The farm boy, who had seen the houseboat, and who was hurrying toward her, waved his hand as Bert called to him. Then, as he came nearer across the green meadow through which the creek ran, he shouted:

"Plenty of fish all around you. Just throw in from the boat, and you'll get all you want."

"What kind of bait do you use?" asked Mr. Bobbsey, for neither Bert nor Harry had thought to inquire about that, and the right kind of bait is as much needed in catching fish, as is water itself.

"Grasshoppers are best just now," answered Will.

"And we've been fishing with worms!" said Bert. "No wonder!"

"Oh, worms are all right most times," Will went on. "But the fish are hungry for grasshoppers now. I'll give you some. I've got lots left."

He came to the edge of the creek, and Mr. Bobbsey, who was steering the boat, sent it in close to shore.

"We might as well tie up here for the night, I think," he said. "That will give you boys a chance to talk to Will, and learn how to catch fish."

A little later the houseboat was rubbing along the grassy bank, and the water was so deep close to shore that there was really no need of putting out the board, called the "gangplank," for any one to get off. Mr. Bobbsey, knowing that Flossie and Freddie could not make the little jump needed to take them ashore, called to Captain White to run out a small board instead of the regular large one.

"Come on, Harry!" called Bert. "We'll get some of those grasshoppers."

He started down the stairs leading from the deck, intending to go ashore, but his mother touched him on the arm, and said, in a low voice:

"Why don't you ask that boy to come on board?"

"Why?" asked Bert.

"Well, I was just going to give you children some of the corn muffins Dinah has just baked, and perhaps Will would like---"

"Oh, of course! Now I understand!" cried Bert. "Of course. I say, Will!" he went on, calling down from the upper deck, "can't you come aboard? We're going to have some of Dinah's corn muffins, and maybe you'd like to sample one."

Somewhat to the surprise of Mrs. Bobbsey, as well as to the wonderment of Bert and Harry, Will did not seem eager to accept the invitation.

"I'd like to come on board, very much," he said, looking back of him, and on all sides, as though he feared some one was after him. "But you see I haven't got much time. I ought to be back at the farm now. Mr. Hardee set me to hoeing a patch of corn, and I'm supposed to be back in time to feed the horses before supper. And it's almost supper time now."

"Well, we don't want you to be late," said Mrs. Bobbsey. "Here, Bert," she said, as Dinah came out of the kitchen with a big plate of muffins, "you take some of these to Will, and you can walk along a little way with him, and talk about fishing. Then he won't be late.

"But don't go too far," she added, "for supper will soon be ready."

"We won't!" promised Bert. Taking some of the delicious corn muffins, the two boys hurried ashore, Snap, the dog, barking joyously, bounding along with them. Flossie and Freddie did not care to go ashore just then, as the little girl twin was playing with her doll, and her brother was trying to make Snoop do one of the tricks that the circus lady had taught the cat in Cuba.

Mrs. Bobbsey went down to the dining-room, to talk to Dinah about the evening meal, while Mr.

Bobbsey and Captain White got out the ropes with which to tie the houseboat fast to some trees on the bank of the creek.

Meanwhile Bert and Harry walked along with Will.

"Have some muffins," invited Bert politely, passing his new friend some of the corn cakes that Dinah knew so well how to bake.

"Thanks! They're good!" said Will, as he bit into one.

"Say, you have some fine fish!" exclaimed Harry, half enviously. "Where'd you catch them?"

"Oh, up the creek aways--near where I was hoeing corn. You can have 'em, if you want 'em."

"What! Do you mean to give them to us?" asked Bert in surprise. "After all the work you had catching them?"

"Oh, it wasn't any work catching 'em," said Will quickly. "It was fun. But it won't be any fun taking 'em home, for Mr. Hardee will be mad."

"Why?" asked Harry, as he began eating a second muffin.

"Well, he'll say I was catching fish instead of hoeing corn. But I caught all these in the noon hour, when I'm supposed to have a little time off. But he wouldn't believe that, so there's no use taking the fish home. You can have 'em. There's some pretty big sunnies, and a couple o' nice perch."

"Sure you don't want them?" asked Bert.

"No. I'd be glad to give 'em to you. And here's some grasshoppers I didn't use. They'll be good to fish with to-morrow."

"Thanks," said Bert, as he took the tin box Will held out. Inside could be heard a queer little "ticking" noise, as the grasshoppers leaped up against the cover.

"Say, these are sure some fine fish!" exclaimed Will.

"Oh, you'll catch just as nice ones to-morrow," the country boy said. "I'll have to run now, or I'll be late at the farm."

"Good-bye!" called Bert and Harry as Will hurried off along the edge of the creek. "See you to-morrow, maybe."

Will had no idea that he would see his friends then. He knew he had a hard day's work in prospect for the next day--weeding a large patch of onions that were so far away from the creek that he would have no chance, even at his noon hour, of going down to the water for a cool little swim.

Will did not know what queer things were going to happen to him very soon, nor did any of the Bobbseys realize what a part they were to play in the life of poor, friendless Will Watson.

"He's a nice boy, isn't he?" asked Harry of Bert, as they turned back toward the boat, with their fish and bait.

"Yes, I like him a lot. It's too bad he has to work so hard on the farm."

"Yes, it sure is."

Talking of the luck they expected to have the next day, fishing, the cousins soon reached the Bluebird. There they found their father and Captain White waiting for them.

"We've decided to move the boat farther down the creek before we tie up for the night," said Mr. Bobbsey, "but we didn't want to go before you boys came back."

"Are you going to start up the engine again?" asked Bert. "If you are, I wish you'd let me try to do it."

"No, you are too small to go near gasoline motors," said his father. "Besides, we are not going to use the engine. We'll just push the boat along with poles from the bank. We're not going very far, but your mother thought it would be nicer to spend the night in a more open place."

"Yes," said Mrs. Bobbsey, "I thought perhaps some animals might jump out of the trees on our deck."

The trees on shore were very close to the boat, some of the branches overhanging the railing. At the mention of animals, Bert's eyes opened wider.

"Say, if I had a gun I could shoot them, if they came aboard," he said, his eyes glistening.

"Nonsense!" exclaimed his mother. "I'd rather have an animal on board than let you have a gun. You might get shot."

"I--I could squirt water on 'em with my fire engine!" shouted Freddie, who had given up trying to make Snoop do any tricks.

"Oh, we had enough of your engine, little fat fireman," said Mr. Bobbsey with a laugh. "Now then, if you're all ready, we'll move the boat."

It was rather hard work to start the Bluebird, but once it had begun to move, it went more easily through the water. Captain White had one pushing pole, Mr. Bobbsey another, and Bert and Harry used one between them. Soon the houseboat moved out from the narrow part of the creek, and from under the trees, to a place where wide meadows were found on either side. A little farther, going around a bend in the stream, the Bobbseys came in sight of a farmhouse, a barn and several other buildings near it.

"Oh, look!" cried Nan. "Somebody lives there."

"Yes, that's Mr. Hardee's farm, I think," said Mr. Bobbsey. "We can tie up our boat here, and then, if we want some milk or eggs, we can easily get them."

"I needs some aigs," spoke Dinah. "Done used de lastest one in dem muffins."

"Then we'll make the boat fast here," decided Mr. Bobbsey. "With your corn muffins, Dinah, and the fish Will gave us, we'll have a fine supper. As soon as the boat is fast you and Harry can clean the fish, Bert."

Beyond the broad expanse which lay between the wide meadows, the creek had narrowed again opposite the farmhouse and barn. In fact, it was so narrow, that if there had been another houseboat on the stream, there would have been trouble for the Bluebird to pass. This narrow part was not, however, very long, and beyond it the creek broadened out again.

Mr. Bobbsey and Captain White had just finished fastening the ropes from the boat to some stakes driven into the ground, when Mrs. Bobbsey, who had come up from the dining-room, called out:

"Oh, look, Richard!"

"What is it?" asked her husband.

"That man! See! I'm afraid he is going to give that boy a whipping. And see, it's Will--the boy who gave Bert the fish!"

Mr. Bobbsey looked to where his wife pointed, and saw, coming out of the barn, a grizzled farmer, leading by the arm a boy whom Mr. Bobbsey at once recognized as Will Watson. Keeping a tight grip on the lad's arm with one hand, the farmer raised his other hand, in which was a long horsewhip.

Then he cried:

"I'll teach you to waste your time goin' fishin'! I'll teach you! Th' idea o' fishin' when I set you to hoein' corn! Wastin' my time! I'll learn you!"

"Oh, but, Mr. Hardee!" cried poor Will. "I only fished in the noon hour when I'm not supposed to work!"

"Not supposed to work!" cried the mean man, as he brought the whip down on Will's shoulders. "You're supposed t' work here all th' while I tell you--'cept when you're asleep! I'll teach you!" and again the cruel whip swished down.

"Oh, Richard!" cried Mrs. Bobbsey faintly, as she covered her eyes with her hands. "Can't you stop that?"

Chapter XII

The Wire Fence

Mr. Bobbsey did not waste any time talking. With a run and a jump he was on shore, and then he started across the meadow toward the place where the mean farmer was whipping Will, who was crying out loud. For the cruel whip hurt.

"Hold on a minute, Mr. Hardee!" exclaimed Mr. Bobbsey, when he was near enough to make himself heard. Back on the deck of the houseboat Mrs. Bobbsey, the twins, their cousins and Dinah watched and waited to see what would happen.

"You talkin' to me?" sharply demanded the mean farmer of Mr. Bobbsey.

"Yes, Mr. Hardee. I asked you to wait a minute before you keep on whipping that boy. I happened to hear part of what he said, and I think he is in the right."

"In th' right? What do you mean?"

"I mean I think he tells the truth, when he says he fished only during the noon hour. We saw him as he came along, and he gave the fish he had caught to my boy."

"Oh, he did, hey?" exclaimed Mr. Hardee. "I was wonderin' what become of 'em. Give 'em away, did he? Wa'al, he knowed better'n to bring 'em here. I knowed he'd been wastin' his time. When I set a boy to hoein' corn, an' he comes home smellin' of fish, I know what he's been doin' jest th' same as when I see a boy's head wet on a hot day I know he's been in swimmin'! You can't fool me. He's frittered away his time, when he ought t' be hoein' corn, an' now I'm goin' to take it out of him!"

Again he raised the whip, and struck the boy.

"Oh, please don't!" begged Will. "Honest I didn't fish except at noon hour, an' I ate my lunch in one hand, and fished with the other, so I wouldn't waste any time. I only took half an hour, instead of three- quarters you said I could have at noon, and I went right to work hoein' corn again."

"Humph! That's easy enough to say," spoke Mr. Hardee, "but I don't believe you. I told you I'd whip you if you went fishin' ag'in, an' I'm goin' to do it!"

Again the lash fell.

"Please don't!" begged Will, trying to break loose. But the angry farmer held him in too firm a grip.

"Look here!" exclaimed Mr. Bobbsey with flashing eyes. "I believe that boy is telling the truth!"

"Wa'al, I don't," snapped the mean farmer. "An' I'm goin' to give him a good lesson."

"Not that way, Mr. Hardee!" cried Mr. Bobbsey, taking a step forward.

"Huh! You seem to know my name," said the farmer, stopping in his beating of the boy, "but I don't know you."

"My name is Bobbsey," said the twins' lather, and the farmer started. "I'm in the lumber business over at Lakeport. I guess you bought some lumber of me, didn't you, for your house."

"Wa'al, s'posin' I did?" asked Mr. Hardee. "I paid you for it, didn't I?"

"Yes, I think so."

"Wa'al, then that don't give you no right to interfere with me! This is my hired boy, an' I can do as I please with him."

"Oh, no, you can't, Mr. Hardee!" said Mr. Bobbsey quickly.

"What's that? I can't? Wa'al, I'll show you! Stand back now, I'm goin' to give him a good threshin'!"

Again he raised the whip, but it did not fall on poor, timid, shrinking Will. For Mr. Bobbsey snatched it away from the angry farmer's hand and flung it far to one side.

"Here! What'd you mean by that?" demanded Mr. Hardee, his face more flushed than ever with anger.

"I mean you're not going to beat that boy!" replied the twins' father. "He hasn't done anything to deserve it, and I'm not going to stand by and see him abused. Is he your hired boy?"

"I took him out of the poorhouse--nobody would hire him. He's bound out to me until he's of age, an' I can do as I please with him."

"Oh, no, you can't," said Mr. Bobbsey. "I happen to know something of the law. You have no right to beat this boy, and if you try to do it now, or again, and I hear of it, I'll make a complaint against you. Don't you strike him again, especially when he hasn't done anything."

Mr. Hardee seemed so surprised that he did not know what to say. His grip on Will's arm slipped off, and Will quickly stepped to one side. There were tears in his eyes, and on his face.

"I believe this boy was telling the truth," said Mr. Bobbsey. "Even if he did fish a little during the time you call yours, that would be no excuse for using a horsewhip on him."

"I tell you he's bound out to me, and I can. do as I please with him!" cried Mr. Hardee.

"No, you can't," said Mr. Bobbsey. "You have no right to be cruel, even if he is a poor boy, and is bound out to you. Haven't you any folks, Will?" he asked.

"No--no, sir," was the half-sobbed answer. "No near folks. I come from th' poorhouse, just as he says. But I've got an uncle somewhere out west. He's a miner. If he knew where I was, he'd look after me."

"Where is your uncle?" asked Mr. Bobbsey.

"I--I got his address, but I can't write very good, or I'd send him a letter."

"Let me have his address," went on Mr. Bobbsey. "And I'll see what I can do."

"Look here!" cried the farmer. "I won't have you interferin' in my business! You ain't got a right to!"

"Every one has a right to stop a poor boy from being unjustly beaten," said the twins' father. "Will, you get me that address. I'll be here a day or so, in my houseboat, and you can bring it down to me. Do you think you can find it, and let me know where your uncle lives?"

"Yes, sir."

"Then do it."

"Now you look-a-here!" began Mr. Hardee, "I won't have you, nor anybody else, interferin' with my hired help. I---"

"I'm not interfering except to stop you from horsewhipping a boy," said Mr. Bobbsey. "Any one has a right to do that."

"Humph!" was all the farmer said, as he over and picked up the horsewhip Mr. Bobbsey had taken from him. The twins' father thought perhaps the farmer was going to use it again, but he did not. Mr. Hardee turned to Will and said:

"Get along up to the house, and eat your supper! There's lots o' work to be done afore dark. An' if I catch you fishin' any more, I'll make you---"

"But I wasn't fishin' except at the noon hour," the boy interrupted.

"That's enough of your talk!" the farmer cried as he walked toward the barn. "Go on!"

Mr. Bobbsey went back to the houseboat.

"It's all right," he said cheerfully to his wife and children. "I made him stop hurting Will."

"Did he--did he hit him very hard?" asked Freddie, for punishment of that sort was totally unknown in the Bobbsey home. Of course the children did not always do right, but they were punished by having some pleasure taken away from them, and never whipped.

"No, Will wasn't much hurt," said Mr. Bobbsey, for he did not want his children, or their cousins, to worry too much over what they had seen. Yet Mr. Bobbsey could not help but think that the cruel lash must have hurt Will more than the boy himself showed.

"He--he won't whip him any more, will he?" asked little Flossie.

"No, not any more," said Mr. Bobbsey, for he had made up his mind he would, if necessary, take the boy away from the mean farmer before any more whipping could be done.

"Suppah am ready!" called Dinah from the kitchen. "An' I done wants yo' all t' come right away fo' it gits cold!"

"We're coming!" cried Mrs. Bobbsey. "And after supper we'll sit on deck and sing songs."

She wanted to do something to take out of the minds of the children the memory of the unpleasant scene they had just observed.

"I wish it would hurry up and come morning," said Bert.

"Why?" asked his father.

"So Harry and I can go fishing. I'm sure we'll catch some with the grasshoppers for bait."

"Well, I hope you have good luck," laughed Mr. Bobbsey.

The supper was much enjoyed. The fish, which Will had given the Bobbseys, made a fine meal, with the corn muffins and other things Dinah cooked. After supper they all sat out on the deck of the houseboat, enjoying the beautiful June evening. From the farm of Mr. Hardee came the sounds of mooing cows, and whinnying horses, with an occasional grunt of the pigs, or the barking of dogs.

Nothing was seen of the farmer himself, or of poor Will.

"Can you do anything for him?" asked Mrs. Bobbsey of her husband, after the children had gone to bed that night.

"I hope so, yes. If, as he says, he has an uncle somewhere in the West, and I can get his address, I'll write to him, and ask him to look after Will. The boy needs a good home."

"Indeed he does. Oh, I'm so glad you didn't let him get that whipping!"

"I'll help him all I can," promised Mr. Bobbsey.

The twins' father rather hoped that the hired boy might slip down to the houseboat that evening, with his uncle's address, but nothing was seen of him.

In the morning a strange thing happened.

Mr. Bobbsey and Captain White decided that it would be better to take the boat a little farther down Lemby Creek, and tie it fast to the bank in a more shady spot than the one opposite the farm buildings.

"It will be better fishing in the shade, too," Mr. Bobbsey said to the boys.

So the gasoline engine was started, and the boat started off. It had not gone very far, though, before Mr. Bobbsey, who was steering, called to Captain White to shut off the engine.

"What's the matter?" asked Captain White. "You're going farther than this; aren't you?"

"I wanted to, yes. But we can't go any farther."

"Why not?" asked Mrs. Bobbsey. "Nothing has happened to the boat, has there, Richard?"

"No, not to the boat. But look there!" and Mr. Bobbsey pointed ahead. Stretched across a narrow part of Lemby Creek was a strong wire fence, fastened to posts driven into the bottom of the stream. The Bluebird could go no farther on her voyage. The fence stopped her.

As Mr. Bobbsey, the twins and the cousins looked at the strong wire fence, they saw Mr. Hardee come along the shore. He looked at the houseboat, and shook his fist, grinning in no pleasant fashion.

"I guess you won't go no farther!" he cried. "I've put a stop to your fancy trip all right! Huh!"

Chapter XIII

The Runaway Boy

"Oh, papa, can't we go on to Lake Romano?" asked Nan, as she came up on deck with Dorothy, and saw the big wire fence stretched across the creek to stop them.

"It doesn't look so--unless we can fly over that," and her brother Bert pointed to the metal strands that went from post to post.

"It does seem to hinder us," said Mr. Bobbsey. He was trying to think of what would be best to do. He looked at Mr. Hardee, who seemed to think it all a fine joke.

"Papa, I know how we can get through," eagerly said little Freddie, who was holding Snoop in his arms. The big black cat was almost too much of a load for the little boy, but Freddie wanted her to do some tricks, and he held her so she would not run away.

"I know how to get past that fence," the little twin went on.

"How?" asked his father, rather absentmindedly. "How?"

"Just cut the wires!" said Freddie, as though no one but himself had thought of that. "If I had one of those cutter-things the telephone man had, when he climbed the pole in front of our house, I could cut the wires and we could go right on up the creek."

"Yes, I suppose so, my little fat fireman," said Mr. Bobbsey. "But I don't believe the man who put that fence up there would let us cut the wires."

"It's queer," said Mrs. Bobbsey. "That fence wasn't across the creek before, was it?"

"I don't know," answered her husband. "It looks as though it had been put up lately--even last night, perhaps. But I haven't been along the creek in some time, so I can't be sure."

"It wasn't here last week, that's certain," Captain White spoke. "For I was up here then fishing, and I didn't see it. I fancy that Mr. Hardee knows something about it."

"I shouldn't wonder," agreed Mr. Bobbsey. "Now the question is: What are we to do? We can't go on through the fence, and we can't very well go around it, for the Bluebird won't float on dry ground. And I don't want to go back. This is the only way to get to Lake Romano."

"I know what to do, papa," spoke Flossie. "We can ask that man to take down the wires, if Freddie can't cut them with the cutter-thing."

"Yes, I suppose we could do that," Mr. Bobbsey said, slowly.

By this time Mr. Hardee had come closer to the houseboat, which had drifted near to the shore.

"Will you take that fence down, and let us go past?" asked Mr. Bobbsey, as politely as he could.

"No, I won't!" snapped Mr. Hardee in reply. "No!"

"But we want to go on down the creek," explained the twins' father, "and we can't get past the fence."

"I know you can't!" said Mr. Hardee with a chuckle. "That's what I put it up there for. I strung it last night--me and my hired men. I didn't think you'd hear, and you didn't. Give you a sort of surprise, didn't it?"

"It certainly did," and Mr. Bobbsey's voice was stern. "And I want to say that you had no right to stretch that fence across the creek to stop my boat. You had no right!"

"Oh, yes, I had!" said Mr. Hardee with a sneer.

"This is a public creek," went on Mr. Bobbsey.

"Maybe it is, in certain places," said the mean farmer, "but here the creek runs through my land. I own on both sides of it, and I own the creek itself. If I don't want to let anybody go through in a boat, I don't have to."

"Oh, so you own the creek here, do you?" asked Mr. Bobbsey, rather surprised.

"Yes, I do."

"And you aren't going to let us pass?"

"Nope! That's why I strung that fence last night. It's a good, strong fence, and if you run into it, and try to bust it I'll have th' law on ye!"

"Oh, you needn't worry that I'll do anything like that," spoke Mr. Bobbsey. "But why won't you let us pass?"

"Because of what you did last night--interferin' between me and my help. You wouldn't let me give Will Watson the threshin' he deserved, an' I won't let you pass through my creek. I want you to back up your boat, too, and go back where you come from. I own that part of the creek where you are now."

"Come now, be reasonable," suggested Mr. Bobbsey. "I stopped you from beating that boy only because you were in the wrong. If you'll just think it over, you'll say so yourself. And, just for that, you shouldn't stop my boat from going up the creek."

"Well, I have stopped you, and I'm going to keep on stoppin' you!" cried Mr. Hardee, again shaking his fist. "You can't get past my fence. It's a good strong fence."

"I--I could cut it, if I had one of those cutter-things, the telephone man had," said Freddie, in his clear, high voice.

"Hush, Freddie dear," said his mother. "Leave it to papa."

Mr. Bobbsey was silent a moment, and then he went on:

"And so you strung that fence in the night, and won't let my houseboat pass, just because I stopped you from beating that boy?"

"That's it," the mean farmer said. "And for more than that, too."

"What do you mean?" asked Mr. Bobbsey quickly.

"I mean that you made that boy, Will Watson, run away."

"Run away!" exclaimed Mrs. Bobbsey, in surprise.

"Yes, run away," repeated the farmer. "He didn't come down to breakfast this mornin', and when I went to call him to do the chores, he was gone. And, what's more, I think you had somethin' to do with him runnin' away," went on the angry farmer. "You put a lot o' notions in his head. You're to blame!"

"Now look here!" exclaimed Mr. Bobbsey. "We don't know any more about that boy running away than you do, Mr. Hardee. If he has gone, I'm sorry for him, for he may have a hard time. I'm not sorry I stopped you from beating him, though. Perhaps he is around the farm somewhere."

"No, he isn't!" insisted the farmer. "He's gone. What clothes he had he took with him. He's run away, and it's your fault, too. I put up that fence last night to pay you back for interferin', an' now I'm glad I did, for you're to blame for Will runnin' off."

"I tell you that you are mistaken," went on Mr. Bobbsey. "But if you feel that way about it, there is no use talking to you. Then you won't take down that wire fence and let us pass?"

"No, I won't, and I order you, and your boat, out of my part of the creek. Go back where you come from. You can't go through to Lake Romano this way!"

Mr. Bobbsey turned and looked at the wire fence. It certainly was a strong one, and the farmer and his hired men had worked well during the night. It was far enough off from where the Bluebird then was so that the pounding on the posts, to drive them into the mud of the creek bottom, was not heard.

"Well, I guess there's nothing for us to do but to go back," said Mr. Bobbsey. He felt very sorry, when he saw the looks of disappointment on the faces of the twins and their cousins.

"Papa," said Freddie again, "if I had one of those wire-cutter things, I could snip that wire like the telephone men did."

"Yes, but we haven't one, little fat fireman, and we would have no right to use it if we had," said Mr. Bobbsey. "No, I must think of some other way."

"It's too bad," said Mrs. Bobbsey. "I wonder what has become of that poor runaway boy?" she asked.

"I don't know," answered Mr. Bobbsey. But, had he only known it, Will Watson was nearer than any one suspected.

Chapter XIV

Off Again

"What are we going to do?" asked Mrs. Bobbsey, as she stood at the side of her husband on the deck of the houseboat. Mr. Bobbsey was looking at the wire fence, as though trying to find a way to get past it--either under it, or over it, or to one side or the other of it. Of course he did not think it wise to try little Freddie's plan of breaking the wire with a "cutter thing" such as the telephone men carried.

"Well," said Mr. Bobbsey, after a bit, "I guess the only thing for us to do is to go back, until we are anchored in some part of Lemby Creek that doesn't belong to Mr. Hardee."

"Does he really own this water?" asked Bert.

"Well, he says so, and I have no doubt but what he does," said Mr. Bobbsey. "If he owns land on both sides of the creek, naturally he owns the creek, too."

"And we can't go up or down it?" asked Mrs. Bobbsey.

"Not unless he lets us."

"What about the fishes?" asked Bert "He can't stop them from swimming up and down."

"No, he can't do that," agreed his father, with a smile.

"Then can he stop Harry and me from catching fish?" Bert wanted next to know.

"Not if you fish somewhere else than in his waters," spoke the twins' father. "The best thing for us to do is to go back where we were at first, near where the creek runs into Lake Metoka. There we can anchor for a time."

"But how are we going to get to Lake Romano?" asked Nan. "I want to show Dorothy the big waterfall."

"Well, perhaps we can get there a little later," her father said. "Just now Mr. Hardee has the best of us, and we'll have to do as he says. So, Captain White, I guess we'll have to back up the boat, as we can't go past the fence."

"If I had one of those wire-cutter things," began Freddie, "I could snip that wire as easy as anything." He seemed to think of nothing else.

"Oh, you and Flossie had better go play with Snap, or Snoop," suggested Bert with a laugh. "Or you can come and watch Harry and me fish. We're going to as soon as we get back aways."

"I'm going to fish, too," declared Freddie, eagerly.

The creek, near Mr. Hardee's farm, was so narrow that the houseboat could not be turned around in it, and it had to go backward. This was easy, since the Bluebird was something like a ferry boat, built to go backward or forward.

The twins were a little sad as they saw their boat backing up, but it could not be helped.

"We'll have a good time fishing, anyhow," said Harry.

"That's right," agreed Bert. "I wonder if that boy Will took his fishing rod with him? He'd probably need it, if he has run away, and is going out west to find his uncle."

"Why would he need a fish-rod?" asked Nan.

"To catch fish to eat," her brother said. "He'll have to have something, and fish are the easiest to get. I almost wish I had gone with him. It will be lots of fun."

"Oh, but it will be very hard, too," said Mrs. Bobbsey. "Think of the lonely nights he'll have to spend, and perhaps with no place to sleep, but on the hard ground. And when it rains---"

"I guess I'll stay home!" laughed Bert, as though he had ever had an idea of running away from home.

Slowly the Bluebird made her way backward until she had passed some posts near the edge of the water. These posts marked the boundary line of Mr. Hardee's farm. He did not own beyond them, and Captain White said the creek was public property there.

"Then we'll anchor here," decided Mr. Bobbsey, as he steered the houseboat toward shore. "Then I think I'll take a little trip back to Lakeport."

"And leave us alone?" cried Mrs. Bobbsey.

"Only for a short while. I want to see some friends of mine, and find out if Mr. Hardee really has the right to fence off Lemby Creek. I don't believe he has."

"Will you be back to-night?"

"Oh, yes. It isn't far to Lakeport. I can walk across the fields and go by trolley."

"I do hope you can find some way of getting past the fence," said Mrs. Bobbsey. "It would be too bad to have our trip spoiled."

As Mr. Bobbsey was getting ready to go back to town, Dinah came out of the dining-room, looking rather puzzled.

"What is the matter?" asked Mrs. Bobbsey. "Are you worried because we can't get those eggs from Mr. Hardee?"

"Well, yessum, dat's partly it," said the fat cook. "We's got t' hab eggs, an' other things too."

"Bert and Harry can walk to the village," said Mr. Bobbsey. "It isn't far from here. I'll go part way with them. So don't worry, Dinah."

"Oh, dat isn't all dat's worryin' me, Massa Bobbsey. But did yo' say de chillums could hab dem corn muffins whut was left over?" and she looked at Mrs. Bobbsey.

"The corn muffins that were left over?" repeated the twins' mother. "No, I said nothing about them. And they know they should not eat between meals without asking me. Why, are the muffins gone, Dinah?"

"Yessum; fo' ob 'em. I put 'em on a plate on de dinin' room table, but now dey's gone."

"Maybe Snap took them," suggested Mr. Bobbsey. "Snoop wouldn't, for she doesn't like such things. But Snap is very fond of them."

Freddie, who heard the talk, hurried over to where the dog was lying asleep in a patch of sunlight, and opened his mouth.

"No, Snap didn't take 'em," said Freddie. "There aren't any crumbs in his teeth."

"Well, maybe you can tell that way, but I doubt it," laughed Mr. Bobbsey. "Perhaps you forgot where you put the muffins, Dinah, or maybe there were none left."

"Oh, I'se shuah I done put 'em on de table," said the fat cook, "an' I'se shuah dey was some left. I'll go look some mo', though."

As there were a few other things besides eggs that were needed for the kitchen of the houseboat, Bert and Harry planned to take a basket, and go to the nearest village store for them. They would walk across the fields with Mr. Bobbsey.

"We'll fish when we come back," said Bert.

"And get enough for dinner and supper," added Harry.

"Better get enough for one meal first," suggested Nan, with a laugh.

The houseboat was now made fast to the bank of the creek some distance away from the wire fence Mr. Hardee had stretched across the stream. It was not to be seen, nor were the farm buildings. The last the Bobbseys had observed of the farmer was as he stood near his wire fence, shaking his fist at the houseboat.

Mr. Bobbsey did not just know how he was going to get past the fence with the Bluebird, or how he could get Mr. Hardee to cut the wire. The twins' father decided to ask the advice of some friends.

Meanwhile Bert and Harry had reached the store, and had brought the eggs, and other groceries, back to Dinah.

"Did you find those corn muffins?" asked Bert.

"Because, if you did, Harry and I would like some. May we have one, mother?"

"If Dinah has them, yes."

"But I cain't find 'em!" complained the fat cook. "Dem muffins hab jest done gone an' hid de'se'ves."

"Oh, I guess we ate them up without knowing it," Bert said, with a laugh. "Never mind, Dinah, a piece of cake, or pie will do just as well."

"Go 'long wif yo'!" cried the cook with a laugh. "I'se got suffin else t' do 'cept make cake an' pies fo' two hungry boys. Yo' jest take a piece ob bread an' butter 'till dinnah am ready."

"All right," agreed Bert. "It won't be long until twelve o'clock. Come on, Harry, and we'll see what luck we have fishing."

"I'm ready," was Harry's answer.

"I'll get you the bread and butter," offered Nan, and she did, adding some jam to the bread, which was a delightful surprise to the two boys.

"I want to fish, too," said Freddie.

"All right, I'll fix you a line," offered Bert. "But be careful you don't fall in. A fish might pull you overboard."

Soon the three boys were dangling their lines over the rail of the Bluebird, while Nan helped her mother with some of the rooms, which, even though they were on a boat, needed "putting to rights." Dinah was busy in the kitchen.

By this time Mr. Bobbsey had reached Lakeport by the trolley. He was going to his lumber office, thinking some of his friends, whom he might call on the telephone could suggest a way out of the trouble. Before he reached the lumber yard, however, he met an acquaintance on the street, a Mr. Murphy.

"Why, hello, Mr. Bobbsey!" exclaimed Mr. Murphy. "I thought you were off on a vacation with your family in a houseboat."

"I was," said the lumber merchant, "but I came back."

"Back so soon? Didn't you like it?"

"Oh, yes, first rate. But we can't go any farther."

"Can't go any farther? What's the matter, did your boat sink?"

"No, but we're stuck in Lemby Creek. Mr. Hardee, a farmer who owns land on both sides of the creek, has put a wire fence across to stop us from going on to Lake Romano."

"Is that so! Well, that's too bad. How did it happen?"

"I'll tell you," said Mr. Bobbsey.

Then he told the story of stopping the angry farmer from beating Will Watson, and how the fence had been built in the night.

"Well, that certainly was a mean trick on the part of Mr. Hardee," said Mr. Murphy. "And so the boy ran away?"

"Yes, and Mr. Hardee accused me of knowing something about him, but I don't--any more than you do."

"I suppose not. But now the question is, How are you going to get past that wire fence?"

"I don't know. The only way I see is to get Mr.

Hardee to cut it, or take it down, and he says he won't do either."

"Humph! Let me see. There ought to be a way out of it. I believe he has the right, as far as the law goes, to put that fence up, but no one else would be so mean. I guess we'll just have to force him to cut those wires, as your little boy, Freddie, suggested."

"Yes, but how can we do it?" asked Mr. Bobbsey. "Mr. Hardee is very headstrong, and set in his ways."

"Let me see," spoke Mr. Murphy slowly, "isn't his name Jake Hardee?"

"Yes, I believe it is."

"And didn't he buy from you the lumber to build his house?"

"Yes, I sold him the lumber, but he paid me for it," said Mr. Bobbsey. "I couldn't get any hold on him that way. He paid for the lumber in cash."

"Yes," cried Mr. Murphy, "but he got the money from me to pay you, and he hasn't paid me back. He still owes me the money, and he gave me a mortgage on his house as security. I've got a hold on him all right. He owes me some interest money, too."

I might say to you little children that when a man wants to build a house and has not enough money, he goes to another man and borrows cash, just as your mamma sometimes borrows sugar, or tea, from the lady next door.

When the man borrows money to build his house, he gives to the man who lends him the cash, a piece of paper, called a mortgage. That paper says that if the man who borrowed the money does not pay it back, and also pay interest for the use of it, the man who lent him the money can take the house. The house is "security" for the loaned money.

It is just as if your mamma went next door to borrow a cup of sugar, and said:

"Now, Mrs. Jones, if I don't pay you back this sugar, and a little more than you gave me, for being so kind as to lend it to me--if I don't pay it back in a week, why you can keep my new Sunday hat." And your mamma might give Mrs. Jones a Sunday hat as "security" for the cup of sugar. Of course ladies do not do those things, but that is what a mortgage is like.

"Yes." said Mr. Murphy to Mr. Bobbsey, "Mr. Hardee borrowed from me the money to buy from you the lumber for his house. And he hasn't paid me back the money, nor any interest on it. I think I'll go up and have a talk with him. And, when I get through talking, I guess he'll let you go through his wire fence."

"I hope he will," said Mr. Bobbsey, "for it would be too bad to have our trip spoiled."

"I'll go right back with you," offered Mr. Murphy.

So it happened that Mr. Bobbsey, with his friend, reached the houseboat, in Lemby Creek, shortly after dinner.

"Oh, back so soon?" asked Mrs. Bobbsey. "What are you going to do, Mr. Murphy?"

"Have a talk with Mr. Hardee."

Mr. Bobbsey and Mr. Murphy walked down the bank of the creek to the farm. They found Mr. Hardee mending a broken harness.

"Mr. Hardee," said Mr. Murphy, "I hear you have

put a wire fence across Lemby Creek, so my friend, Mr. Bobbsey, can't get past with his houseboat."

"Yes, I have," growled the farmer, "and that fence is going to stay up, too! I'll show him he can't come around here, interferin' with me when I try to punish my help. He made Will run away too."

"No, I did not. I know nothing of him," said Mr. Bobbsey.

"Mr. Hardee," went on Mr. Murphy. "I want you to take down that fence, and let the houseboat go on up the creek."

"And I'm not going to!"

"Very well, then," said Mr. Murphy, quietly, "perhaps you are ready to pay me the interest on my mortgage which has been due me for some time, Mr. Hardee."

The farmer seemed uneasy.

"Well, to tell you the truth," he said, "I haven't got that money just now, Mr. Murphy. Times have been hard, and crops are poor, and I'm short of cash. Can't you wait a while?"

"I have waited some time."

"Well, I'd like to have you wait a little longer. I'll pay you after a while."

"And I suppose you'll take down that wire fence, and let Mr. Bobbsey and the twins go past--after a while?"

"Well--maybe," growled the mean farmer.

"Maybe won't do!" exclaimed Mr. Murphy. "I want you to take the wire fence down right away."

"Well, I'm not going to do it. He interfered with

me, and made that boy run away, and I'm not going to let him go up my part of the creek."

"Well, then, Mr. Hardee, if you can't do something for Mr. Bobbsey, as a favor, I can't do anything to oblige you. Mr. Bobbsey is a friend of mine and unless you cut your wire fence, I'll have to foreclose that mortgage, and take your house in payment for the money you owe me. That's all there is about it. Either pay me my money--or cut that fence. It must be one or the other."

Mr. Hardee squirmed in his seat, and seemed very uneasy.

"I--I just can't pay that money," he said.

"Then I'll have to take your house away."

"I--I don't want you to do that, either."

"Then cut the wire fence!" cried Mr. Murphy.

"Wa'al, I--I guess I'll have to," said Mr. Hardee, but it was clearly to be seen that he did not want to. He went into the barn, and came out wearing a pair of rubber boots, and carrying a pair of pincers-- the "wire-cutting things," as Freddie called them.

Wading out into the creek Mr. Hardee snipped the wires of the fence.

"There, now you can go on," he said to Mr. Bobbsey, but his tone was not pleasant.

"I thought I knew how to make him give in," whispered Mr. Murphy.

"Thank you," said Mr. Bobbsey to his friend. They hurried back to the houseboat.

"We're going on again!" cried the twins' father. "The fence is down."

"Oh, fine!" said Bert.

"Now for the waterfall!" sighed Nan, who loved beautiful scenery.

"Oh, I've caught a fish!" suddenly shouted Freddie and he jumped about so that his mother, with a scream, ran toward him, fearing he would go overboard.

Chapter XV

Overboard

"Look out, Freddie!"

"Be careful there, little fat fireman!"

Thus Mrs. Bobbsey cried to the small twin, and thus Mr. Bobbsey also warned his son, who had pulled up his pole with a jerk, when he felt a nibble on the fishline.

"I'll look out for him!" cried Bert, and he got between his little brother and the railing of the boat, so there would be no danger of Freddie's falling overboard. Freddie had no intention of getting into the water, but he was much excited over his fish.

"I caught it all myself!" he cried. "I caught a fish all by myself, and nobody helped me. Didn't I, Bert?"

"Yes, Freddie, except that Harry put on the grasshopper bait."

"But where's the fish?" asked Nan, who, as yet, had not seen one.

"Here it is!" cried Freddie, as he ran toward the end of his line which lay on deck. "I caught a fish, and it's all mine--every bit," and he held up a little, wiggling sunfish which, somehow or other, had been caught on the tiny hook.

"Oh, it's a real, live fish!" squealed Flossie, dropping her doll to get a better view of this new plaything. "Are we going to have it for supper, Freddie?"

"No!" cried the little fat fellow, as he tried to hold the fish up by the swinging line in one hand, and grasp it in the other. The fish was so slippery that, every time Freddie had it, his hand slid off of it. "We're not going to eat my fish!" cried Freddie. "I'm going to keep it forever, in a glass globe, and make it do tricks!"

The others gathered around to see Freddie's catch, for the little fellow was very proud of his success, though, once or twice before, on trips to the country, he had been allowed to fish with Bert and Nan. He was too impatient to sit still long, so he never caught much.

"Here comes Snoop," said Mr. Bobbsey, with a laughing glance at his friend Mr. Murphy, who had come back to the houseboat with him, after the mean farmer had cut the wire fence.

"Snoop can't have my fish!" cried Freddie, now hugging his dangling prize close to his waist.

"Oh, you'll get your clothes all dirty!" cried Mrs. Bobbsey, as the black cat came snooping and sniffing around, for she smelled fish, which she very much liked.

"Go 'way, Snoop! You can't have my fish!" cried Freddie. "I'm going to put it in a glass globe, and keep it forever and teach it to do tricks."

"I guess swimming is the only trick a fish can do," said Bert, with a laugh, "and you don't have to teach them that. They know it already."

Freddie was so afraid that Snoop might get his fish, that Dinah brought him up a glass dish, in which, when it was filled with water, the little "sunny" was allowed to swim around. The hook had become fastened in only a corner of the mouth, and the fish was not hurt in the least.

Freddie was as proud as though he had caught a whale or a shark. He did not care to fish any more, but stood on deck near the box on which had been placed the dish containing his fish.

Bert and Harry, who had caught some larger fish, went back to their rods and lines, while Nan took up Freddie's pole and used it for herself. Flossie divided her time between getting her doll to "sleep" and watching Freddie's fish.

"Well, are we really going up the creek?" asked Mrs. Bobbsey.

"Yes, Mr. Murphy got the farmer to cut the wire fence, so we can get past," said Mr. Bobbsey. "We had better start, too, for Mr. Hardee might change his mind, and put back the wire fence."

"I guess there isn't much danger of that," spoke Mr. Murphy. "But you have a fine boat. I don't wonder that you didn't want to stay cooped up here in this creek."

Flossie, who had come over near the visitor, said:

"There's a stove in our kitchen, and Dinah cooks things on it--good things to eat!"

"Does she?" cried Mr. Murphy, catching the little girl up in his arms. "That's fine!"

"I think you might take that as an invitation to dinner," said Mrs. Bobbsey, with a laugh.

"Thanks, I will stay, and see how it feels to eat on board a houseboat," replied the man who had helped Mr. Bobbsey.

Bert and Harry decided that they had caught enough fish now, so they pulled in their lines, and soon the Bluebird was moving slowly up the creek, toward Lake Romano, though it would be a day or so before the Bobbseys reached it.

As the houseboat went past the wire fence, which had been cut, the twins and their cousins looked at it in wonder. Only the posts stood there now, and there was room enough between them for the houseboat to pass. A little way back from the shore stood Mr. Hardee.

"I'm not going to let every boat go past that wants to!" he called to Mr. Bobbsey. "I'll let you through, as a favor to Mr. Murphy, but I'm not going to have a whole lot of them sailin' up and down my creek!"

"Just as if it would hurt the water," said Bert, in a low voice.

They were all glad when a turn of the stream hid Mr. Hardee from sight. The mean farmer evidently thought he had not been unpleasant enough, for he ran after the houseboat a little way, crying:

"If you see anything of that good-for-nothing boy of mine, I want you to tell him to come back here, or it will be the worse for him."

"We're not likely to see him," said Mr. Bobbsey.

"I don't know about that," went on the farmer. "I believe you folks know something about him."

"That's all nonsense!" said Mr. Bobbsey, sharply. "I've told you we don't know where he is, and haven't

seen him since you tried to horsewhip him. That ought
to be enough."

"Wa'al, we'll see," was the growling answer, as the
mean farmer turned away.

The houseboat kept on, until it was well past Mr.
Hardee's land, and then, in a pleasant part of the creek,
it was tied to the bank. Dinah served supper.

"See! I told you we had a stove, and that Dinah
could cook things," said Flossie, as a plate full of
steaming hot corn muffins was set on the table.

"So you did, my dear!" exclaimed Mr. Murphy, who
sat next to the little "fat fairy."

Flossie seemed to think the most wonderful part
of the houseboat was the kitchen and the stove.

When the pleasant meal was over, they sat on deck
in the evening, until it was time for Mr. Murphy to go
home. He was to walk across the meadow, about a mile,
to get a trolley car. Mr. Bobbsey went with him, part of
the way.

For several days after this, the Bobbsey twins had all
sorts of amusements on the house-boat. The Bluebird
was still kept in the creek, for it was so pleasant there,
along the shady waterway, that Mrs. Bobbsey said they
might as well enjoy it as long as possible.

"But I want to see the big lake and the waterfall,"
said Nan.

"We'll soon be there," promised her father.

One day the houseboat was moved along the creek
for about a mile, and anchored there. Bert and Harry
found the fishing so good, that they wanted to stay a
long time. They really caught some large perch and
chub.

"But we didn't come on this trip just to fish," said Mr. Bobbsey. "There are other things to do. We want to go in swimming, when it gets a little warmer, and then, too, we can take some walks in the woods on the shores of Lake Romano."

"And can we have picnics, and take our lunch?" asked Freddie.

"Yes, little fat fireman," answered his father, laughing.

Freddie had been kept so busy with other amusements, that he had not once played with his fire engine, since coming on board.

"Let me catch some fish," begged Flossie, on the afternoon of the day when they were to move from the place that Bert and Harry liked so well.

"You may take my line," offered Freddie. "I'm tired of fishing."

I think perhaps Freddie grew weary because he had had no bites. That one fish he had caught, and which had caused so much excitement, seemed to be all he could get. That one was still alive in the glass dish, which Bert had made into sort of an aquarium.

"I'm going to catch a big fish," said Flossie, as she laid her doll down beside the sleeping dog Snap, and took Freddie's pole.

"Don't fall in--that's all," cautioned Mrs. Bobbsey.

"I'll watch her," offered Dorothy, for Nan had gone down to help dry the dishes, it being her "turn."

Somehow or other, every one forgot Flossie for a moment, and even Dorothy, who had promised to watch her, forgot when she saw some small boats, filled with young folks on an excursion, pass the houseboat.

Suddenly there came a scream from little Flossie.

"I see him! I see him!" she cried. "He's on our boat!"

The next moment her mother, who turned quickly as she heard Flossie's voice, saw the little girl lean far over the rail of the Bluebird. Then came a splash. Flossie had fallen overboard!

Chapter XVI

The Missing Sandwiches

"Flossie is in the water!"

"Get the boat!"

"Snap! Jump in and get her!"

"Oh, Flossie!"

So many were the excited cries that followed the falling over the rail of little Flossie, that no one could tell who was speaking, or crying out.

Harry, who was near the rail, turned sharply as he heard the splash, and then, quickly casting off his coat, he gave a clean dive over the side. Harry was a country boy, and had learned to swim when very young. He was not at all afraid of the water, and, more than once, he had pulled from "the old swimming hole," boys smaller than himself, who had gone beyond their depth, and could not get out.

"I'll get her!" cried Harry, as he dived over the side.

"Oh, it's all my fault!" sobbed Dorothy. "I said I'd watch her. But I forgot! It's all my fault!"

"No, it isn't, dear!" said Nan, quickly putting her arms around her cousin. "Flossie does things so quickly, sometimes, that no one can watch her. But we'll get her out, for the water isn't deep."

It was deep enough though, on that side of the boat, to be well over Flossie's head, and of course, plunging down from the height she did, she at once went under water.

Snap seemed to understand what had happened, and to know that his services were needed, for he gave a bark, and made a rush for the rail.

"Don't let him jump in!" cried Mr. Bobbsey to Bert. "If Harry can get her, Snap might only make trouble. Hold him back, Bert, while I get the rowboat."

Mrs. Bobbsey, with one arm around Freddie, had rushed to the rail to look down. She saw Flossie come to the surface, choking and gasping for breath, and then saw Harry, who had gone under, but who had come up again, strike out for the little girl.

"Oh, save her!" gasped Mrs. Bobbsey.

"He will!" said Bert. "Harry's a fine swimmer. Come back, Snap!" he called to the big dog, getting his hands on his collar, just in time, for Snap was determined to go to the rescue himself. He whined, pulled and tugged to get away from Bert.

"Help me hold him!" cried Bert to Nan.

"I will!" she answered, glad to be doing something. Together the two older Bobbsey twins managed to keep Snap back. Dorothy, too, helped, for Snap was very strong.

"Did Flossie go after a fish?" asked Freddie, and he asked it in such a queer way that it would have caused a laugh at any other time. Just now every one was too frightened to laugh.

After all, there really was not so much danger. Mr. Bobbsey had taught Flossie some of the things one must do when learning to swim, and that is to hold your breath when you are under water. For it is the water getting into the lungs that causes a person to drown. After her first plunge into the creek, the little girl thought of what her father had told her, and did hold her breath.

"I--I'll get you!" called Harry to her. "Don't be afraid, Flossie! I'll get you!"

Flossie was too much out of breath to answer, so she did not try to speak. Harry was soon at her side, and called to her:

"Now put your hands on my shoulders, Flossie, and I'll swim to the boat with you. Don't try to grab me around the neck."

Harry knew how dangerous it was for a person trying to rescue another in the water to be choked. Flossie was a wise little girl, even if she was not very old. She did as her cousin told her, and, with Flossie's hands on his shoulders, Harry began to swim toward the Bluebird.

He did not have to go very far, though, for by this time Mr. Bobbsey and Captain White were there with the rowboat, and the two children were soon lifted in. They were safe, and not harmed a bit, except for being wet through.

"Oh, Flossie, whatever did you do it for?" asked her mother, when she had hugged the dripping little girl in her arms. "Why did you do it?"

"Do what, mamma?" Flossie asked.

"Lean over so far."

"I wanted to see if I had a fish," went on Flossie. "And I had to lean over. And then I saw him."

"Saw whom?" asked her father. "What do you mean?"

"Why, I saw him--that boy," and Flossie seemed surprised that her father did not understand.

"What boy?" asked Mrs. Bobbsey. "Did you fall asleep there, Flossie, and were you dreaming, when you fell in?"

"No, mamma. I didn't fall asleep. I saw him, I tell you."

"I heard her say something about seeing some one, just as she went over the rail, head first," Dorothy said.

"But whom do you mean, Flossie?" asked puzzled Mrs. Bobbsey.

"Why, that boy--the one the bad man whipped."

"Oh, Will Watson!" exclaimed Bert. "Where did you see him, Flossie? Was he in one of the excursion boats that went past?"

"No, he was on our boat--down there," and Flossie pointed straight down. "I saw him!" she declared.

"I guess she must have dozed off a little, and dreamed it," spoke Mr. Bobbsey, with a smile. "That was it. The sun was so hot, that she just slept a little as she was fishing. She might have had a bite, and that awakened her so suddenly that she gave a jump and fell over the rail. I must have it built higher. Then there won't be any danger."

"Yes, do," said Mrs. Bobbsey. "We've had scares enough."

"But I did see that boy--the one that gave Bert the fish," insisted Flossie. "He was on our boat. I saw him as plain as anything."

"It must have been some one in the excursion boats that looked like him," spoke Nan.

"No, I saw Will!" declared the little twin, and, rather than get her excited by disputing, they allowed her to think she really had seen a strange face, as she leaned over.

"But of course she either dreamed it, or saw some one she thought was that runaway boy," Mr. Bobbsey said, afterward. "It's all nonsense to think he was on our boat."

Snap, who had not been allowed to go to the rescue, much as he had wanted to, leaped about Flossie, barking and wagging his tail in joy.

"Anybody would think he'd done it all," said Bert. "Say, Harry, you're all right! That was a dandy dive!" and he clapped his cousin on the back.

"Indeed we never can thank you enough. Harry," said Mrs. Bobbsey, and tears of thankfulness glistened in her eyes.

"Oh, it wasn't anything at all," the country boy said, modestly blushing, for he did not like such a "fuss" made over him. "I knew I could get her out."

"Well, it was very fine of you," said Mr. Bobbsey, warmly. "Now then, you had better change your clothes, for, though it is summer, you might take cold. And Flossie, too, must change."

"Yes, I'll look after her," said her mother "Now remember, little fat fairy," Mrs. Bobbsey went on, giving Flossie her father's pet name, "you must never lean over the rail again. If you do---"

"But I saw---" began Flossie.

"No matter what you saw--don't lean over the rail!" said her mother. "If you do, we shall have to give up this houseboat trip."

This seemed such a dreadful thing, that Flossie quickly promised to be very careful indeed.

"But I did see him, all the same!" she murmured, as her mother took her to the bedroom to change her clothes. "I saw that boy on our boat."

The others only laughed at Flossie for thinking such a queer thing.

"That poor boy is far enough away from here now," said Bert. "I wonder if he will really try to make his way out west?"

"I don't know," answered Harry, who had changed to a dry suit, hanging his other in the sun to let the water drip out of it. "I've read of boys making long journeys that way."

"I wouldn't want to try it," spoke Bert.

"Neither would I," said his cousin. "This houseboat suits me!"

Flossie was little the worse for her accident, and was soon playing about again with Snoop and Snap, and with Freddie. The little fellow and his sister made the dog and cat do many tricks.

It was the day after this, when the Bluebird had gone a little farther up the creek, that Mrs. Bobbsey planned a little picnic on shore. They were not far from a nice, green forest.

"We'll have Dinah put us up a little lunch, and we'll go in the woods and eat it," said Mrs. Bobbsey.

"Oh, that will be fun!" cried Nan. "Won't it, Dorothy?"

"Indeed it will," said the seashore cousin.

"I'm going to take my doll," Flossie said. "There's no water in the woods for her to fall in, is there, mamma?"

"No, not unless you drop her into a spring," laughed Mrs. Bobbsey.

"I'll see if Dinah has finished making the sandwiches," offered Nan. "She had them almost finished a little while ago."

But when Nan went to the dining-room, she found the colored cook very much excited.

"What is the matter, Dinah?" asked Nan.

"Mattah! What am de mattah?" Dinah repeated, "Dey's lots de mattah, Missie Nan."

"Why, what can it be?"

"De sandwiches is gone, dat's what's de mattah!"

"The sandwiches, Dinah?"

"Yes'm, de sandwiches what I done make fo' de excursnick!"

"Oh, you mean for our picnic, Dinah?"

"Yes'm, dat's it. Excursnick I calls it. But de sandwiches I done jest made am gone. I s'pects Massa Bert or his cousin done take 'em fo' fun."

"Oh, no, Dinah. Bert nor Harry wouldn't do that. Are you sure you made the sandwiches?"

"I'se jest as shuah, Missie Nan, as I am dat I'se standin' heah. I'se jest as shuah as I is dat time when I made de corn cakes, an' somebody tuck dem! Dat's how shuah I is! Dem sandwiches what was fo' de excursnick am done gone completely."

"But have you looked everywhere, Dinah?" asked Nan.

"Eberywhere! Under de table an' on top ob de table. I had dem sandwiches all made an' on a plate. I left dem in de dinin' room to go git a basket, an' when I come back, dey was gone entirely. I want t' see yo' ma, Missie Nan. I ain't gwing t' stay on dish yeah boat no mo, dat's what I ain't!"

"But why not, Dinah?" asked Nan, in some alarm.

"Because dey's ghostests on dish yeah boat; dat's what dey is! An' I ain't gwine stay on no ha'nted boat. Fust it were de corn cakes, an' now it's de sandwiches. I'se gwine away--I ain't gwine stay heah no mo'!"

Chapter XVII

In the Storm

Dinah was certainly very much frightened, but Nan was not. She knew better than to believe in such things as "ghosts," and, though the sandwiches might have disappeared, the little girl felt sure there must be some reasonable explanation about the mystery.

"I'll call mamma, Dinah," offered Nan. "She won't want you to leave us now, when we have just started on this trip."

"Go on, honey lamb, call yo' ma," agreed the fat cook. "But I ain't gwine t' stay on dish yeah boat no mo'! Dat's settled. Call yo' ma, honey lamb, an' I'll tell her about it."

Mrs. Bobbsey had heard the excited voice of Dinah and had come down to the dining-room of the houseboat to see what it was all about.

"What is it, Dinah?" she asked.

"It's ghostests, Mrs. Bobbsey--dat's what it is," said the cook. "Ghostests what takes de sandwiches as fast as I make 'em--dat's de trouble. I can't stay heah no mo'!"

Mrs. Bobbsey looked to Nan for an explanation. The little girl said:

"Dinah made a plate of sandwiches for our picnic—"

"Dat's right, for de excursnick," put in Dinah.

"And she left them on the table," went on Nan. "But when she went to get a basket to put them in, and came back—"

"Dey was clean gone!" burst out the colored cook, finishing the story for Nan. "An' ghostests took 'em; ob dat I'se shuah. So you'd bettah look fo' anoder cook, Mrs. Bobbsey."

"Nonsense, Dinah! We can't let you go that way. It's all foolishness to talk about ghosts. Probably the door was left open, and Snap might have taken the sandwiches, though I never knew him to take anything off the table. But it must have been Snap."

"No'm, it couldn't be," said Dinah. "It wasn't Snap."

"How do you know?"

"Could Snap come through a closed do', Mrs. Bobbsey. Could Snap do that?"

"Come through a door? No, I don't believe he could. But he might open it. Snoop can open doors."

"Yes, maybe do's that hab a catch on, but not knob-do's, Snoop can't open, an' Snap can't neither. Besides, de do' was shut when I left de sandwiches on de table an' went fo' de basket."

"Oh, was it?" asked Mrs. Bobbsey, trying to think of how the pieces of bread and meat could have been taken.

"It shuah was," went on Dinah. "Nobody took dem

sandwiches, but a ghostest, an' I can't stay in no boat what has ghostests."

"Nonsense!" laughed Mrs. Bobbsey. "I know how it was done, Dinah. I know how the sandwiches were taken."

"How, Mrs. Bobbsey?" asked the colored cook, as she stood looking first at the empty plate on the table, and then at Nan and lastly at Mrs. Bobbsey.

"Why, through that window," said the twins' mother, pointing to an open window on the side of the Bluebird. "Snap must have come in that window, and taken the sandwiches. He was probably very hungry, poor dog, though he knows better than to do anything like that." "No'm, Mrs. Bobbsey," went on Dinah. "Snap couldn't hab come in fru dat window, fo' it opens right on to de watah. He'd hab to stand in de watah to jump in, an' he can't do that."

"No, perhaps not," admitted Mrs. Bobbsey. "Oh, I dare say you forgot where you put the sandwiches, Dinah. Now don't worry a bit more about them. Just make some fresh ones, and we'll go on our little picnic."

"But I'se gwine t' leab," said Dinah. "I ain't gwine stay on a boat, where ghostests takes sandwiches as fast as I can make 'em."

"You shall come with us on the picnic," said Nan's mother. "When we come back, there won't be any ghost. Now don't fuss. Just make some fresh sandwiches, and we'll go. I'm sure it was Snap."

"And I'se shuah it were a ghostest," murmured Dinah, as she went out to the kitchen.

"Mamma, who do you think it could have been?" asked Nan of her mother.

"Why, Snap, to be sure, little daughter."

"But with the door shut, and the window opening out on the water?" went on Nan.

"Oh, dogs are very smart," said Mrs. Bobbsey. "Smarter than we think. Now suppose you help Dinah make more sandwiches. We are late."

Nan went out to the kitchen, while Mrs. Bobbsey made her way up on deck, where she found her husband talking to Captain White about the motor engine of the houseboat.

"Richard, I want to speak to you," said Mrs. Bobbsey, and when she and the twins' father were in a quiet corner of the deck, Mrs. Bobbsey went on:

"Richard, I think there are thieves about here."

"Bless my soul!" he exclaimed. "Thieves! What do you mean?"

"Well, I mean that Dinah says a plate of sandwiches was just taken, and you remember the time the corn muffins were missing?"

"Yes, but perhaps Dinah was mistaken both times, or Snap might have taken a bite between meals."

"Hardly Snap this time," Mrs. Bobbsey went on, "and Dinah, though she does forget once in a while, would not be likely to do so twice in such a short time. No, I think some tramps along shore must have come along quietly in a boat, reached or climbed in through the window and taken the sandwiches."

"Well, perhaps they did," Mr. Bobbsey, said. "I'll tell Captain White, and we'll keep a lookout. We don't want thieves coming around."

"No, indeed," said Mrs. Bobbsey. "Dinah threatens to leave, if any more queer things happen."

"Well, we wouldn't know how to get along without Dinah," said Mr. Bobbsey, with a smile. "I'll put some wire netting over the windows. I was going to do it anyhow, for the mosquitoes will soon be buzzing around. The netting will keep thieves from reaching in and taking our nice sandwiches."

"Yes, I think the netting would be a good idea," said his wife. "But it certainly is queer."

A little later, the Bobbsey twins--both sets of them--with their cousins, mother, father, and Dinah went ashore for the little picnic in the woods, taking with them the fresh sandwiches that Nan had helped to make.

"You shan't have any of these--at least not until we want you to have them," said Nan to Snap, the dog, who, of course, was not left behind. Yet, the more she thought of it the more sure Nan was that Snap had not taken the others.

"But, if he didn't, who did?" she wondered.

"Oh, isn't it just lovely in these woods!" exclaimed Dorothy, as they walked along on the soft moss under the trees. At the seashore, where she lived, the woods were too far away to allow her to pay many visits to them, and she always liked to walk in the cool forests.

Harry, though he lived in the country, not far from the woods, liked them as well as did the Bobbsey twins, and the children were soon running about, playing games, while Snap raced about with them, barking and wagging his tail.

Dinah sat down near the lunch basket.

"Don't you want to walk around a bit?" asked Mrs. Bobbsey.

"No'm," answered the fat cook. "I ain't gwine t' leab dish yeah basket ob victuals until dey's eaten. Dey ain't no ghostests, nor no dogs, gwine t' git nothin' when I'se heah! No'm!" and Dinah slipped her fat arm in through the handle of the basket.

"Let's look for chestnuts!" cried Freddie. "I love chestnuts!"

"It's too early for them," said his father. "But if you find me a willow tree, I can make you some whistles."

The children found one, near a little brook, and Mr. Bobbsey was soon busy with his knife. The bark slipped off easily from the willow wood, which is why it is so often used for whistles.

Soon all four children were blowing whistles of different tones, and making so much noise that, with the barking of Snap, who seemed to think he must bark every time a whistle was blown, Mrs. Bobbsey cried out for quietness.

"Come on, we'll go farther off in the woods and play Indian," suggested Bert, and soon this game was under way.

It was lunch time almost before the children knew it, and what fun it was to sit around the table cloth Dinah spread out on the grass, and eat the good things from the basket. Snap was given his share, but Snoop, the black cat, had not come along, staying on the houseboat with Captain White.

"Isn't this fun?" cried Nan to Dorothy.

"Indeed it is! Oh, I can't tell you how glad I am that you asked me to come on this trip!"

"Oh! Look at that big bug!" suddenly cried Freddie, and he made a jump toward his mother, to get out of the way of a big cricket that had hopped onto the white table cloth.

"Look out, Freddie!" called his father. "You'll upset your glass of lemonade!"

Mr. Bobbsey spoke too late. Freddie's heel kicked over the glass, and the lemonade spilled right into Mrs. Bobbsey's lap.

"Oh, Freddie!" cried Bert.

"Never mind--it's an old dress," laughed Mrs. Bobbsey, "and there's more lemonade. Accidents will happen on picnics. Never mind, Freddie."

The cricket was "shooed" away by Nan, Freddie's glass was filled again, and the picnic went on merrily. Soon it was time to go back to the boat.

As they walked along through the woods, Mr. Bobbsey glanced up now and then through the trees at the sky.

"Do you think it's going to rain?" his wife asked.

"Not right away, but I think we are soon going to have a storm," he said.

"Oh, well, the houseboat doesn't leak, does it?"

"No, but I don't want to go out on Lake Romano in a storm, and I intended this evening to go on up the creek until we reached the lake. But I'll wait and see what the weather does."

"Well, did anything happen while we were gone?" asked Mrs. Bobbsey of Captain White, as they got back to the houseboat.

"No, not a thing," he answered. "It was so still and quiet here, that Snoop and I had a nice sleep," and he pointed to the black cat, who was stretched out in his lap, as he sat on deck.

As it did not look so much like a storm now, Mr. Bobbsey decided to move the houseboat farther up the creek, almost to where the stream flowed from Lake Romano, so as to be ready to go out on the larger body of water in the morning, if everything was all right.

The engine was started, and just before supper, the Bluebird came to a stop in Lemby Creek about a mile from the big lake. She was tied to the bank, and then supper was served.

Then followed a pleasant hour or two on deck, and when it was dark, the children went into the cabin and played games until bedtime--Nan and Bert, as well as the smaller twins and the cousins, were asleep when Mrs. Bobbsey, who had sat up to write some letters, heard her husband walking about on deck.

"What are you doing?" she called to him through a window.

"Oh, just looking at the weather," he answered. "I think we're going to have a storm after all, and a hard one, too. I'm glad we're safely anchored."

Sure enough. That night, about twelve o'clock, the storm came. There was at first distant, muttering thunder, which soon became louder. Then lightning followed, flashing in through the windows of the houseboat, so that Mrs. Bobbsey was awakened.

"Oh, it's going to be a terrible storm," she said to her husband.

"Oh, perhaps not so very bad," he answered. "Here comes the rain!"

Then it began to pour. But the houseboat was well built, and did not leak a bit.

Next the wind began to blow, gently at first, but finally so hard that Mr. Bobbsey could hear the creaking of the ropes that tied the boat to trees on shore.

"I think I'd better look and see if those ropes are well tied," he said, getting up to dress, and putting on a raincoat.

He had hardly gotten out on deck, before the houseboat gave a sudden lurch to one side, and then began to move quickly down stream.

"Oh, what has happened?" cried Mrs. Bobbsey.

At the same time Flossie and Freddie awakened, because of the loud noise from the storm.

"Mamma! Mamma!" they cried.

"Richard, has anything happened?" asked Mrs. Bobbsey.

"Yes!" he shouted. "The strong wind has broken the ropes, and we are adrift. But don't worry. We'll soon be all right!"

Faster and faster went the Bluebird, while all about her the rain splashed down, the wind blew, the thunder roared, and the lightning flashed.

Chapter XVIII

Strange Noises

The frightened cries of Flossie and Freddie soon awakened Nan and Bert, and it was not long before Harry and Dorothy, too, had roused themselves.

"What's the matter?" asked Bert.

"Oh, we've gone adrift in the storm," his mother said. "But don't worry. Papa says it will be all right."

"Come up on deck and see what's going on!" cried Bert to Harry.

He had begun to dress, and now he thrust his head out from his room. "Hurry up, Harry," he added. "We want to see this storm."

"No, you must stay here," Mrs. Bobbsey said. "It is too bad a storm for you children to be out in, especially this dark night. Your papa and Captain White will do all that needs to be done."

"Mamma, it--it isn't dark when the lightning comes," said Freddie. He did not seem to be afraid of the brilliant flashes.

"No, it's light when the flashes come," said his mother. "But I want you all to stay here with me. It is raining very hard."

"I should say it was!" exclaimed Harry, as he heard the swish of the drops against the windows of the houseboat.

"Is Snap all right, mamma?" asked Flossie. "And Snoop? I wouldn't want them out in the storm."

"They're all right," Mrs. Bobbsey said.

"Oh, what's that!" suddenly cried Nan, as the houseboat gave a bump, and leaned to one side.

"We hit something," Bert said. "Oh, I wish I could go out on the deck!"

"No, indeed!" cried his mother. "There! They've started the engine. Now we'll be all right."

As soon as Mr. Bobbsey had found out that the houseboat had broken loose from the mooring ropes in the storm, he awakened Captain White, and told him to start the motor.

This had been done, and now, instead of drifting with the current of the creek, the boat could be more easily steered. Soon it had been run into a sheltered place, against the bank, where, no matter how hard the wind blew, it would be safe.

"Are we all right now?" asked Mrs. Bobbsey, as her husband came down to the cabin.

"Yes, all right again," he said. "There really was not much danger, once we got the motor started."

"Is it raining yet?" asked Freddie, who was sitting in his mother's lap, wrapped in a sweater.

"Indeed it is, little fat fireman," his father answered. "You wouldn't need your engine to put out a fire to-night."

The patter of the raindrops on the deck of the

houseboat could still be heard, and the wind still blew hard. But the thunder and lightning were not so bad, and gradually the storm grew less.

"Well, we'd better get to bed now," said Mr. Bobbsey. "To-morrow we shall go to the big lake."

"Did the storm take us far back down the creek?" asked Bert.

"Not more than a mile," said his father.

"And the man can't tie us in with wire again, can he?" Freddie wanted to know. "If he does, and I had one of those cutter-things, I could snip it."

"You won't have to, Freddie," laughed Bert.

"Speaking of that mean farmer reminds me of the poor boy who ran away from him," said Mrs. Bobbsey to her husband, when the children had gone to bed. "I wonder where he is to-night, in this storm?"

"I hope he has a sheltered place," spoke the father of the Bobbsey twins.

Not very much damage had been done by the storm, though it was a very hard one. In the morning the children could see where some big tree branches had blown off, and there had been so much rain, that the water of the creek was higher. But the houseboat was all right, and after breakfast, when they went up the creek again, they stopped and got the pieces of broken rope, where the Bluebird had been tied before.

The houseboat then went on, and at noon, just before Dinah called them to dinner, Nan, who was standing near her father at the steering wheel, cried:

"Oh, what a lot of water!"

"Yes, that is Lake Romano," said Mr. Bobbsey.

"We'll soon be floating on that, and we'll spend the rest of our houseboat vacation there."

"And where shall we spend the rest of our vacation?" asked Bert, for it had been decided that the houseboat voyage would last only until about the middle of August.

"Oh, we haven't settled that yet," his father answered.

On and on went the Bluebird, and, in a little while, she was on the sparkling waters of the lake.

"I don't see any waterfall," said Freddie, coming toward his father, after having made Snap do some of his circus tricks.

"The waterfall is at the far end of the lake," said Mr. Bobbsey.

"I wonder if there are any fish in this lake?" spoke Bert.

"Let's try to catch some," suggested his cousin Harry, and soon the two boys were busy with poles and lines.

The Bobbsey twins, and their cousin-guests, liked Lake Romano very much indeed. It was much bigger than the lake at home, and there were some very large boats on it.

Bert and Harry caught no fish before dinner, but in the afternoon they had better luck, and got enough for supper. The evening meal had been served by Dinah, Snap and Snoop had been fed, and the family and their guests were up on deck, watching the sunset, when Dinah came waddling up the stairs, with a queer look on her face.

"Why, Dinah! What is the matter?" asked Mrs. Bobbsey, seeing that something was wrong. "Have you lost some more sandwiches?"

"No'm, it ain't sandwiches dish yeah time," Dinah answered. "But I done heard a funny noise jest now down near mah kitchen."

"A funny noise?" repeated Mr. Bobbsey. "What was it like?"

"Jes like some one cryin'," Dinah answered. "I thought mebby one ob de chilluns done got locked in de pantry, but I opened de do', an' dey wasn't anybody dere. 'Sides, all de chilluns is up heah. But I shuah did heah a funny noise ob somebody cryin'!"

Mrs. Bobbsey looked at her husband and said:

"You'd better go see what it is, Richard."

Chapter XIX

Snap's Queer Actions

The Bobbsey twins looked at one another. Then they glanced at their cousins, Harry and Dorothy. Next the eyes of all the children were turned on fat Dinah.

"Was--was it a baby crying?" Freddie wanted to know.

"Yes, honey lamb--it done did sound laik a baby-- only a big baby," explained the colored cook.

"Maybe it was one of Flossie's dolls," the little "fat fireman" went on.

"Flossie's dolls can't cry!" exclaimed Nan. "Not even the one that says 'mama,' when you punch it in the back. That can't cry, because it's broken."

"Well, Flossie says her dolls cry, sometimes," said Freddie, "and I thought maybe It was one of them now."

"It was Snoop, our cat," said Bert, with a laugh. "That's what you heard, Dinah, Snoop crying for something to eat. Maybe she's shut up in a closet."

"Probably that's what it was, Dinah," said Mrs. Bobbsey.

"I'll go let her out," said Mr. Bobbsey, starting toward the lower part of the houseboat.

"'Scuse me, Mr. Bobbsey," said Dinah firmly, "but dey ain't no use yo' going t' let out no cat Snoop."

"Why not, Dinah?"

"Because it wasn't any cat dat I done heah. It was a human bein' dat I heard cryin', dat's what it was, an' I know who it was, too," the colored woman insisted.

"Who, Dinah?" asked Mrs. Bobbsey.

"It was de same ghostest dat done took mah cakes an' sandwiches, dat's who it was. I'se mighty sorry t' leab yo', Mrs. Bobbsey, but I guess I'll done be goin' now."

"What, Dinah!" cried her mistress. "Going? Where?"

"Offen dish yeah boat, Mrs. Bobbsey. I cain't stay heah any mo' wif a lot of ghostests."

"Nonsense, Dinah!" exclaimed Mr. Bobbsey. "There isn't any such thing as a ghost, and you know it! It's silly to even talk about such a thing. Now you just come with me, and show me where you heard those noises."

"No, sah, I cain't do it, Mr. Bobbsey," the colored cook exclaimed, moving backward.

"Why not?" Mr. Bobbsey wanted to know.

"'Cause it's bad luck, dat's why. I ain't goin' neah no ghostest---"

"Don't say that again, Dinah!" exclaimed Mrs. Bobbsey sharply, with a glance at the children.

"Oh, we're not afraid, mother!" chimed in Bert. "We know there's no such thing as a ghost."

"That's right," spoke his father. "But, Dinah, I

must get this matter settled. It won't do for you to be frightened all the while. You must come and show me where you heard the noise."

"Has I got to do it, Mrs. Bobbsey?" asked Dinah.

"Yes, I think you had better."

"Well, den, I heard de noise right down in de passageway dat goes from de kitchen to de dinin' room. Dat's where it was. A noise laik somebody cryin' an' weepin'."

"And are you sure it wasn't Snoop, Dinah?"

"Shuah, Mr. Bobbsey. 'Cause why? 'Cause heah's Snoop now, right ober by Miss Dorothy."

This was very true. The little seashore Cousin had been playing with the black cat.

"Snap howls sometimes," said Freddie, who seemed to be trying to find some explanation of the queer noise. "Lots of times he used to howl under my window, and I'd think it was some boy, but it was only Snap. He used to like to howl at the moon."

"Dat's right, so he does, honey lamb," Dinah admitted. "But dere ain't no moon now, an' Snap's eatin' a bone. He don't never howl when he's eatin' a bone, I'se sartain ob dat."

"Oh, well, if it wasn't the dog or cat, it was some other noise that can easily be found," said Mr. Bobbsey. "I'll go have a look."

"I'm coming, too," said Nan.

"And so am I!" exclaimed Bert.

Harry and Dorothy looked at each other a moment, and then Dorothy said, rather unhesitatingly:

"I'm not afraid!"

"I should say not!" cried Mrs. Bobbsey. "What is there to be afraid of, just in a noise?"

"Let's all go!" suggested Harry.

"Good!" cried Mr. Bobbsey, for he wanted his children not to give way to foolish fears. They were not "afraid of the dark," as some children are, and from the time when they were little tots, their parents had tried to teach them that most things, such as children fear, are really nothing but things they think they see, or hear.

"Aren't you coming, Dinah?" asked Mrs. Bobbsey, as they all started for the lower part of the houseboat.

"No'm, I'll jest stay up heah an'--an' git a breff ob fresh air," said the colored cook.

"Come on, children," called Mr. Bobbsey, with a laugh. "We'll very soon find out what it was."

They went down off the deck, to the passageway between the kitchen and dining-room. This place was like a long, narrow hall, and on one side of it were closets, or "lockers," as they are called on ships. They were places where different articles could be stored away. Just now, the lockers were filled with odds and ends--bits of canvass that were sometimes used as sails, or awnings, old boxes, barrels and the like. Mr. Bobbsey opened the lockers and looked in.

"There isn't a thing here that could make a crying noise, unless it was a little mouse," he said, "and they are so little, I can't see them. I guess Dinah must have imagined it."

"Let's listen and see if we can hear it," suggested Mrs. Bobbsey.

All of them, including the children, kept very quiet. Snap, the trick dog, was still gnawing his bone in the kitchen. They could hear him banging it on the floor as he tried to get from it the last shreds of meat. Snoop, the black cat, was up on deck in the sun.

"I don't hear a thing," said Mrs. Bobbsey.

Indeed it was very quiet.

"Hark!" suddenly called Nan. "Isn't that a noise?"

They all listened sharply, and then they did hear a faint sort of crying, or whining, noise.

"Oh!" exclaimed Freddie. "It's a---"

"It's the boat pulling on one of the anchor ropes," said Mr. Bobbsey, for the Bluebird was anchored out in the lake by two anchors and ropes, one at each end. "The wind blows the boat a little," the children's father explained, "and that makes it pull on the ropes, which creak on the wooden posts with a crying noise."

"I know!" exclaimed Flossie. "Just like our swing rope creaks, when it's going slow."

"Exactly," said her mother. Mrs. Bobbsey was glad that the little girl could think out an explanation for herself that way.

"There it goes again!" suddenly exclaimed Bert.

They all heard the funny noise. There was no doubt but that it was the creaking of the rope by which the boat was tied.

"Here, Dinah!" called Mr. Bobbsey, with a laugh. "Come down here. We've found your ghost."

"I doan't want to see it!" exclaimed the colored cook, "Jest toss it overbo'd!"

"It's nothing but a noise made by a creaking rope," said Nan. "And you can't throw that overboard."

"All right, honey lamb. Yo' can call it a rope-noise ef yo' all laiks," said Dinah, when finally she had been induced to come down. "But I knows it wasn't. It was some real pusson cryin', dat's what it was."

"But you said it was a ghost, Dinah!" laughed Bert, "and a ghost is never a real person, you know. Oh, Dinah!"

"Oh, go long wif yo', honey lamb!" exclaimed the fat cook. "I ain't got no time t' bodder wif you'. I'se got t' set mah bread t' bake t'morrow. An' dere's some corn cakes, ef yo' ma will let yo' hab 'em."

"I guess she will," said Bert, with a laugh. "Some cakes and then bed."

They all thought the "ghost" scare was over, but Mr. Bobbsey noticed that when Dinah went through the passage between the kitchen and dining-room, she hurried as fast as her feet would take her, and she glanced from side to side, as though afraid of seeing something.

Every one slept soundly that sight, except perhaps Dinah, but if anything disturbed her, she said nothing about it, when she got up to get breakfast. It was a fine, sunny day, and a little later the Bluebird was moving across the lake, the motor turning the propeller, which churned the blue water into foam.

Mr. Bobbsey steered the boat to various places of interest on the lake. There were several little islands that were to be visited, and on one of the tiniest, they went ashore to eat their lunch.

"Let's play we're shipwrecked," suggested Freddie, who was always anxious to "pretend" something or other.

"All right," agreed Flossie. "You'll be Robinson Crusoe, and I'll be your man Thursday."

"Friday--not Thursday," corrected Freddie, for his father had read to him part of Robinson's adventures.

The little twins were allowed to take some of their lunch, and go off to one side of the island, there to play at being shipwrecked. Mr. and Mrs. Bobbsey sat in the shade and talked, while Nan, Dorothy, Bert and Harry went off on a little "exploring expedition," as Bert called it. Bert was making a collection of stones and minerals that year, and he wanted to see what new specimens he could find.

Suddenly the peacefulness of the little island was broken by a cry of:

"Oh, Mamma! Papa! Come quick! Freddie's in the cave, and can't get out. Oh, hurry!"

"That's Flossie's voice!" cried Mrs. Bobbsey, in alarm.

Mr. Bobbsey did not say anything. He just ran, and soon he came to the place where Flossie and Freddie had gone to play shipwreck. He saw Flossie jumping up and down in front of a little hill.

"Where's Freddie?" asked Mr. Bobbsey.

"In there," Flossie answered, pointing to the pile of dirt that looked to have been freshly dug. "We made a cave in the side of the and Freddie went in to hide, but he dirt slid down on him and he--he's there yet!"

"Gracious!" cried Mr. Bobbsey. "It's a good thing we're here!"

With a piece of board he soon scattered the dirt until he came to Freddie's head. Fortunately the little fellow was covered with only a few inches of the soil, and as a piece of brush had fallen over his face, he had had no trouble in breathing. He was rather badly frightened, however, when he was dug out, little the worse, otherwise, for his adventure.

"What did you do it for?" asked his father, when he and his mother had brushed the dirt from the little chap, while the other children gathered around to look on.

"I--I was making a cave, same as Robinson Crusoe did," Freddie explained. "I dug it with a board in the sand, and I went in--I mean, I went in the cave, and it--it came down--all of a sudden."

"Well, don't do it again," cautioned his mother. "You might have been badly hurt."

They finished their visit on the island, and went back on board the Bluebird again. Snap, who always went with them on these little excursions, bounded on deck, and then made a rush for the kitchen, for he was hungry, and he knew Dinah generally had a bone, or something nice for him.

Mr. Bobbsey, who was following close behind Snap, was surprised to see the dog come to a sudden stop in the passageway between the kitchen and dining-room. Snap growled, and showed his teeth, as he did when some savage dog, or other enemy, was near at hand.

"What's the matter, old fellow?" asked Mr. Bobbsey. "Do you see something?"

Snap turned and looked at Mr. Bobbsey. Then the dog looked at one of the locker doors, and, with a loud bark, sprang toward it, as though he would go through the panels.

Chapter XX

At the Waterfall

"What's the matter?" asked Mrs. Bobbsey, who had followed her husband into the passageway. "Snap and Snoop aren't quarreling, are they?"

"Indeed, no," answered Mr. Bobbsey. "But Snap is acting very strangely. I don't know what to make of him."

By this time Mrs. Bobbsey had come up, where she could see the dog. Snap was still standing in front of the door, growling, whining, and, now and then, uttering a low bark.

"What's the matter with him?" asked Mrs. Bobbsey. "Is he hungry?"

"Well, I guess he's always more or less hungry," her husband said, "but that isn't the matter with him now. I think perhaps he imagines he sees Dinah's ghost!" and he laughed.

"Snap, come here!" called Mrs. Bobbsey, and, though the dog usually minded her, this time he did not obey. He only stood near the door, growling.

"Why don't you open it, and let him see what's in

there," said Bert. "Maybe it's only some of those mice that made the noise," he went on.

"Perhaps it is," his father answered. "I'll let Snap have a chance at them."

As Mr. Bobbsey stepped up to turn the knob of the "locker," or closet door, there was a noise inside, as though something had been knocked down off a shelf. Snap barked loudly and made a spring, to be ready to jump inside the closet as soon as it was opened.

"What's that?" cried Mrs. Bobbsey, while Flossie and Freddie, a little alarmed, clung together and moved nearer to their mother.

"There's something inside there, that's sure," declared Mr. Bobbsey. "It must be a big rat!"

"Mercy!" cried Mrs. Bobbsey. "A rat!"

"I'll have to set a trap," Mr. Bobbsey went on. "That rat has probably been taking the things to eat that Dinah missed--the corn-cakes and the sandwiches."

"That's right!" cried Bert. "That ends the mystery. Go for him, Snap!"

"Bow wow!" barked the dog, only too willing to get in the closet and shake the rat.

But, when Mr. Bobbsey opened the door, no rat ran out, not even a little mouse. Snap was ready for one, had there been any; but though he pawed around on the floor, and nosed behind the boxes and barrels, he caught nothing.

"Where is it?" asked Flossie.

"I want to see the rat!" cried Freddie. Neither of the smaller twins was afraid of animals. Of course, they did not know that rats can sometimes bite very fiercely, or they might not have been nearly so anxious to see one.

"I guess the rat got away," said Mr. Bobbsey, as he watched Snap pawing around in the locker, even pushing aside boxes with his nose.

"Hab yo' cotched de ghost?" asked Dinah, looking out from her kitchen.

"Not yet--but almost," said Mr. Bobbsey. "I must clean out this closet, and find the rat-hole. Then I'll set the trap. Come away Snap. You missed him that time."

The dog was not so sure of this. He stayed near the closet, while Mr. Bobbsey set out the boxes and barrels, but no rat was to be seen, nor even a mouse. And, the odd part of it was that, when everything was out of the locker, there was no hole to be seen, through which any of the gnawing animals might have slipped.

"That's funny," said the twins' father, as he peered about. "I don't see how that rat got in here, or got out again."

"Perhaps it wasn't a rat," suggested Mrs. Bobbsey.

"What was it, then, that made the noise?" asked her husband.

"I don't know," she answered. "Something might have bumped against the boat outside."

"Yes, that's so," admitted Mr. Bobbsey. "But Snap wouldn't act that way just on account of a noise."

The boxes and barrels were put back into the closet, but even that did not seem to satisfy Snap. He remained near the locker for some time, now and then growling and showing his teeth. Mr. Bobbsey looked in some of the other, and smaller, lockers, but all he found was a tiny hole, hardly big enough for a mouse.

"Perhaps it was a mouse," he said. "Anyhow, I'll set a trap there. Dinah, toast me a bit of cheese."

"Cheese, Massa Bobbsey!" exclaimed the colored cook. "Yo' knows yo' cain't eat cheese. Ebery time yo' does, yo' gits de insispepsia suffin terrible--specially toasted cheese."

"I don't intend to eat it!" answered the twins' father, with a laugh. "I'm going to bait a trap with cheese to catch the mice. I don't care whether they get the indigestion or not."

"Oh! Dat's diffunt," said Dinah. "I'll toast yo' some."

The trap was set, but for two or three days, though it was often looked at, no mice were caught. Meanwhile, several times, Dinah said she missed food from her kitchen. It was only little things, though, and the Bobbseys paid small attention to her, for Dinah was often forgetful, and might have been mistaken.

"I really think we have some rats aboard," said Mr. Bobbsey. "There are some on nearly every boat. I have heard noises in the night that could be made only by rats."

"And Snap still acts queerly, whenever he passes that locker," said Mrs. Bobbsey. "I'm not so sure it is a rat that made that noise, Richard."

"No?" her husband asked. "What was it, then?"

But Mrs. Bobbsey either could not, or would not, say.

"I say, Harry," said Bert to his country cousin one day, when the Bluebird had come to anchor some distance down the lake, "let's try to get to the bottom of this mystery."

"What mystery?"

"Why, the one about the noise, and the sandwiches and cakes being taken, and Snap acting so funny. I'm sure there's a mystery on this boat, and we ought to find out what it is."

"I'm with you!" exclaimed Harry. "What shall we do?"

"Let's sit up some night and watch that closet," said Bert. "We can easily do it."

"Will your folks let us?"

"We won't ask them. Oh, I wouldn't do anything I knew they didn't want me to do without asking," Bert said quickly, as he saw his cousin's startled glance.

"But there's no harm in this," Bert went on. "We'll go to bed early some night, and, when all the rest of them are asleep, we'll get up and stand watch all night. You can watch part of the time, and when you get sleepy I'll take my turn. Then we can see whether anything is hiding in that closet."

"Do you think there is?" asked Harry.

"I'm sure I don't know what to think," Bert answered. "Only it's a mystery, and we ought to find out what it is."

"I'm with you," said Harry again.

"Are you talking secrets?" asked Nan, suddenly coming up just then.

"Sort of," admitted her brother, laughing.

"Oh, tell me--do!" she begged.

"No, Nan. Not now," said Bert. "This is only for us boys."

Nan tried to find out the secret, but they would not tell her.

Two days later, during which the Bluebird cruised about on the lake, Bert said to Harry, after supper:

"We'll watch to-night, and find out what's, in that closet. Snap barked and growled every time to-day, that he passed it. I'm sure something's there."

"It does seem so," admitted Harry.

Mr. Bobbsey was steering the boat toward shore, intending to come to anchor for the night, when Flossie, who was standing up in front cried:

"Oh, look! Here's the waterfall! Oh, isn't it beautiful!"

Just before them, as they turned around a bend in the bank, was a cataract of white water, tumbling down into the lake over a precipice of black rocks--a most beautiful sight.

Chapter XXI

What Bert Saw

The waterfall of Lake Romano was still some little distance off, and, as the wind was blowing toward it, only a faint roar of the falling water came to the ears of the Bobbsey twins, and the others on the houseboat.

"Oh, papa!" exclaimed Nan. "May we go close up and see the cataract?"

"Yes," said Mr. Bobbsey. "I intended to give you a good view of the waterfall. We shall spend a day or so here, as it is a great curiosity. There is one place where you can walk right behind the falls."

"Behind it!" cried Harry. "I don't understand how that can be, uncle."

"You'll see to-morrow, when we visit them," said the twins' father. "And there are some oddly-marked stones to be picked up, too, Bert. They will do for your collection."

"Fine!" Bert exclaimed. "Say, this has been a dandy trip all right!"

"It isn't ended yet, is it, Dorothy?" asked Nan.

"No, indeed," replied the seashore cousin, with a smile.

"And we haven't solved the mystery," said Bert in a low voice to Harry. "But we will to-night, all right."

"We sure will," agreed the boy from the country.

The Bobbsey twins stayed up rather later that night than usual. Mr. Bobbsey did not find a good anchorage for the boat for some time, as he wanted to get in a safe place. It looked as though there might be a storm before morning, and he did not want to drift away again. Then, too, he wanted to get nearer to the waterfall, so they could reach it early the next morning and look at it more closely.

So the motor was kept in action by Captain White until after supper, and finally the Bluebird came to rest not far from the waterfall. Then Bert and Nan, with Dorothy and Harry were so interested in listening to Mr. Bobbsey tell stories about waterfalls, and what caused them, that the older twins and their cousins did not get to bed until nearly ten o'clock, whereas nine was the usual hour.

Of course Flossie and Freddie "turned in," as sailors say, about eight o'clock, for their little eyes would not stay open any longer.

"We'll wake up as soon as my father and mother are asleep," said Bert to Harry, as they went to their rooms, which were adjoining ones. "Then we'll take turns watching that closet."

"Sure," agreed Harry. "Whoever wakes up first, will call the other."

To this Bert agreed, but the truth of it was that neither of them awakened until morning. Whether it was that they were too tired, or slept later than usual, they could not tell. But it was broad daylight, when they sat up in their beds, or "bunks," as beds are called on ships.

"I thought you were going to call me," said Bert to his cousin.

"And I thought you were going to call me," laughed the boy from the country.

Then they both laughed, for it was a good joke on each of them.

"Never mind," spoke Bert, as he got up and dressed. "We'll try it again to-night."

"Try what?" asked Nan from the next room, for she could hear her brother speak. "If you boys try to play any tricks on us girls---"

"Don't worry," broke in Harry. "The secret isn't about you."

"I think you're real mean not to tell us!" called Dorothy, from her room. "Nan and I are going to have a marshmallow roast, when we go on shore near the waterfall, and we won't give you boys a single one, will we, Nan?"

"Not a one!" cried Bert's sister.

"Will you give me one--whatever it is?" asked Freddie from the room where his mother was dressing him.

"And me, too?" added Flossie, for she always wanted to share in her little twin brother's fun.

"Yes, you may have some, but not Bert and Harry," went on Nan, though she knew when the time came, that she would share her treat with her brother and cousin.

"Well, I didn't hear any noises last night," said Mr. Bobbsey to his wife at the breakfast table.

"Nor I," said she. But when Dinah came in with a platter of ham and eggs, there was such a funny look on the cook's face that Mrs. Bobbsey asked:

"Aren't you well, Dinah?"

"Oh, yes'm, I'se well enough," the fat cook answered. "But dey shuah is suffin strange gwine on abo'd dish yeah boat."

"What's the matter now?" asked Mr. Bobbsey.

"A whole loaf of bread was tooken last night," said Dinah. "It was tooken right out ob de bread box," she went on, "and I'se shuah it wasn't no rat, fo' he couldn't open my box."

"I don't know," said Mrs. Bobbsey. "Rats are pretty smart sometimes."

"They are smart enough to keep out of my trap," said Papa Bobbsey. "I must set some new ones, I think."

"Well, I don't think it was any rat," said Dinah, as she went on serving breakfast.

There was so much to do that day, and so much to see, that the Bobbsey twins, at least, and their cousins, paid little attention to the story of the missing loaf of bread. Bert did say to Harry:

"It's too bad we didn't watch last night. We might have caught whoever it was that took the bread."

"Who do you think it was?" asked Harry.

"Oh, some tramps," said Bert. "It couldn't be anybody else."

They went ashore after breakfast, close to the waterfall.

"Papa, you said you would show us where we could walk under the water without getting wet," Nan reminded him.

"Oh, yes," said Mr. Bobbsey. "I have never been to these falls, but I have read about them." Then he showed the children a place, near the shore of the lake, where they could slip in right behind the thin veil of water that fell over the black rocks, high above their heads. Back of the falling water there was a space which the waves had worn in the stone. It was damp, but not enough to wet their feet. There they stood, behind the sheet of water, and looked out through it to the lake, into which it fell with a great splashing and foaming.

"Oh, isn't this wonderful!" cried Nan.

"It surely is," said Dorothy, with a sigh. "I never saw anything so pretty."

"And what queer stones!" cried Bert, as he picked up some that had been worn into odd shapes by the action of the water.

The Bobbseys spent some little time at the waterfall, and then, as there was a pretty little island near it, where picnic parties often went for the day, they went there in the Bluebird, going ashore for their dinner.

"But I'm not going to play Robinson Crusoe again," said Freddie, as he remembered the time he had been caught in the cave.

At the end of a pleasant day on the island, the Bobbseys again went on board the houseboat for supper.

"We'll watch sure to-night," said Bert to Harry, as they got ready for bed. "We won't go to sleep at all."

"All right," agreed the country cousin.

It was hard work, but they managed to stay awake. When the boat was quiet, and every one else asleep, Harry and Bert stole softly out of their room and went to the passageway between the dining-room and kitchen.

"You watch from the kitchen, and I'll watch from the dining-room," Bert told his cousin. "Then, no matter which way that rat goes, we'll see him."

"Do you think it was a rat?" asked Harry.

"Well, I'm not sure," his cousin answered. "But maybe we'll find out to-night."

"We ought to have something to hit him with, if we see a rat," suggested Harry.

"That's right," Bert agreed. "I'll take the stove poker, and you can have the fire shovel. Now keep very still."

The two cousins took their places, Bert in the dining-room, and Harry in the kitchen. It was very still and quiet on the Bluebird. Up on deck Snap, the dog, could be heard moving about now and then, for he slept up there.

Bert, who had sat down in a dining-room chair, began to feel sleepy. He tried to keep open his eyes, but it was hard work. Suddenly he dozed off, and he was just on the point of falling asleep, when he heard a noise. It was a squeaking sound, as though a door had been opened.

"Or," thought Bert, "it might be the squeak of a mouse. I wonder if Harry heard it?"

He wanted to call out, in a whisper, and ask his

cousin in the dining- room, just beyond the passage. Bert could not see Harry. But Bert thought if he called, even in a whisper, he might scare the rat, or whoever, or whatever, it was, that had caused the mystery.

So Bert kept quiet and watched. The squeaking noise of the loose boards in the floor went on, and then Bert heard a sound, as though soft footsteps were coming toward him. He wanted to jump up and yell, but he kept still.

Then, suddenly, Bert saw something.

Standing in the dining-room door, looking at him, was a boy, about his own age--a boy dressed in ragged clothes, and in bare feet, and in his hand this boy held a piece of bread, and a slice of cake.

"You--you!" began Bert, wondering where he had seen that boy before. And then, before Bert could say any more, the boy turned to run away, and Bert jumped up to catch him.

Chapter XXII

The Stowaway

"Come back here!" cried Bert, as he rushed on.

There was the sound of a fall in the passageway, and some one groaned.

"What is it?" cried Harry, running from the kitchen. "What's the matter, Bert? Did you catch the rat?"

"No, but I caught something else," Bert answered. By this time he had run into the passageway, and there, in front of the locker, or closet, where the strange noises had been heard, lay the ragged boy. He had fallen and hurt his head. The cake and bread had been knocked from his hands. The door of the locker or closet was open.

"Why--why---" began Harry, in surprise. "It's a--a boy."

"Yes, and now I know who he is," said Bert, as the stowaway sat up, not having been badly hurt by his fall. He had tripped in his bare feet.

"Who--who is it?" asked Harry.

"It's that boy who gave us the fish--Will Watson,

who worked for the man that made the wire fence--Mr. Hardee."

"Yes, I'm that boy," said the other, slowly. "Oh, I hope your folks won't be very mad at me. I--I didn't know what to do, so when I ran away, I hid on your boat."

"And have you been here ever since?" asked Bert.

"Yes," answered Will. "I've been hiding here ever since."

"And was it you who took the things?" Harry wanted to know.

"Yes, I took them. I was half starved. But I'll pay you back as soon as I get out west, where my uncle lives. He's a gold miner, and I guess he's got lots of money. Oh, I hope your father and mother will forgive me."

"Of course they will," said Bert, seeing tears in the eyes of the ragged boy.

"What's the matter there?" called Mr. Bobbsey. "Has anything happened, Bert?"

"Yes," answered Bert. "We've solved the mystery--Harry and I."

"Solved the mystery!" cried Mr. Bobbsey. "I'll be right there."

"Oh, what can it be?" his wife asked.

Meanwhile, Captain White, Dinah and the little Bobbsey twins had been awakened by the loud voices. Up on deck Snap, the dog, feeling that something was wrong, was barking loudly.

"I--I hope the dog doesn't get me!" said Will, looking about.

"I won't let him hurt you," promised Bert. "So it

was you, hiding in the closet that made Snap act so funny?" he asked. "He knew you were there."

"Yes, only I wasn't in the closet all the while. There was a loose board at the back. I could slip out of the closet through that hole. I hid down in the lower part of the boat. I'll show you."

"You poor boy!" exclaimed Mrs. Bobbsey when, with her husband, she had come to see the "mystery," as Bert laughingly called him.

"Indeed we'll forgive you. You must have had a terrible time, hiding away as you did. Now tell us all about it. But first I want you to drink this warm milk Dinah has made for you," for Mrs. Bobbsey had told the cook to heat some. "You look half starved," she said to the boy.

"I am," answered Will. "I--I didn't take any more of your food than I could help, though."

"Yo' am welcome to all yo' want, honey lamb!" exclaimed Dinah. "Mah land, but I shuah am glad yo' ain't no ghostest! I shuah am!" and she sighed in relief, as she saw that Will was a real, flesh-and-blood boy. He was, however, very thin and starved-looking.

"Now tell us all about it," said Mr. Bobbsey. "How did you come on our boat?"

Will told them. After Mr. Bobbsey had stopped the cruel farmer from beating him, Will crawled up to his room to sob himself to sleep. Then he began to think that after the houseboat had gone, Mr. Hardee would probably treat him all the more meanly, on account of having been interfered with.

"So I just ran away," said Will. "I packed up what

few things I had, and when I saw your boat near shore, I crept aboard and hid myself away. I easily found a place down--down cellar," he said with a smile.

"I suppose you mean in the hold, or the place below the lower deck," spoke Mr. Bobbsey. "Cellars on a boat are called 'holds.' Well, what happened?"

"I--I just stayed there. I found some old bags, and made a bed on them," Will said. "Then when my food gave out, I used to crawl out during the nights and take some from your kitchen.

"I had some bread when I ran away," Will went on. "I took it from Mrs. Hardee's kitchen, but they owed me money for working, and I didn't take more bread than I ought."

"I'm sure you didn't," said Mrs. Bobbsey, kindly.

"I didn't want you to know I was on board the boat," Will resumed, "for I was afraid you'd send me off, and I didn't want Mr. Hardee to find me again. I was afraid he'd whip me."

"But what did you intend to do?" asked Mr. Bobbsey.

"Well, I heard you say you were going to Lake Romano," said the boy, "and I thought I would ride as far as you went. Then I wouldn't have so far to walk to get to my uncle out west. I'm going to him. He'll look after me, I know. I can't stand Mr. Hardee any more."

"You poor boy. We'll help you find your uncle," said Mrs. Bobbsey.

"And you've been on board ever since?" asked Mr. Bobbsey.

"Yes, sir. I hid down in the 'hold,' as you call it.

Then when I got hungry, I found a loose board, so I could get into the closet. Then at night I would come out and get things to eat and a little water or milk to drink. I didn't mean any harm."

"No, I'm sure you did not," the twins' father said. "Well, I'm glad Bert found you," he went on, as Bert and Harry told how they had kept watch. "So it was you who took the things, and who made the noises that frightened Dinah?"

"Yes, but I didn't mean, to scare her," Will said. "That day I got my hand caught in the loose board, and it hurt so, and I felt so bad that I--I cried. That was what she heard, I guess."

"You poor boy!" said Mrs. Bobbsey again.

"And--and did you see any rats in the cellar?" asked Freddie, who was moving about in his little night dress.

"No," answered Will, "I didn't see any rats. It was bad enough in the dark place, without any rats."

"Well, I guess your troubles are over, for a time," said Mr. Bobbsey. "We'll fix you up a bed, and then I'll have a talk with you about this miner uncle of yours."

Will finished his warm milk, and ate some bread and cake--the same he had taken from Dinah's kitchen. He had gone in there and taken it, but Harry had not heard him, for Harry had fallen asleep.

"And so it was a stowaway boy, and not rats or ghosts or anything else that was the mystery," said Mrs. Bobbsey, when everything once more quiet on the Bluebird.

"That's what it was," her husband said "Bert was real smart to sit up and watch."

"And he never told us a thing about it."

"Oh, he wanted to surprise us," laughed Mr. Bobbsey.

"And didn't I see you, the time I fell overboard?" asked Flossie, looking at Will.

"I think you did," he laughed. "I happened to put my head out of a ventilating hole just as you looked. I pulled it in again, soon enough, though. I hope I didn't scare you."

"Not very much," Flossie said. "I was sure I saw you, but nobody else would believe me."

Snap soon made friends with the new boy. It was Will, hiding behind the closet wall, that had made the dog act as though a rat were there.

I must bring my story to a close, now that the mystery is explained. And, really, there is little else to tell. Will had, in the little bundle of things he had brought away from Mr. Hardee's with him, the address of a man he thought knew where the miner uncle was. Mr. Bobbsey wrote several letters, and, in due time, word came back that Will's uncle was well off now, and would look after him. His name was Mr. Jackson. He had lost track of Will for some years and had just begun a search for him, when Mr. Bobbsey's letter came. Enough money was sent on to enable Will to make the trip out west, where he would be well cared for. He could not thank the Bobbsey family enough for what they had done for him.

Mr. Hardee heard where his runaway boy had been found, and tried to get him back, but Mr. Bobbsey would not permit this. So Will's life began to be a pleasant one. The time he had spent on the houseboat, after coming from his hiding place, was the happiest he had ever known.

"Well, what shall we do now?" asked Bert one day, after Will had gone. "It seems queer not to have to be on the lookout for a mystery or something like that."

"Doesn't it," agreed Harry.

"And so that was your secret?" asked Nan.

"Yes, that was it," her brother answered. "But I wish we had something to do now."

"Whatever you do, you want to do in the next two weeks," said Mr. Bobbsey, coming up on deck.

"Why?" asked Bert.

"Because our houseboat trip will come to an end then."

"Oh!" cried the Bobbsey twins in a chorus. "That's too bad!"

"But I have other pleasures for you," went on Mr. Bobbsey. "The summer vacation is not yet over."

And those of you who wish to read of what further pleasures the children had, may do so in the following volume, which will be called "The Bobbsey Twins at Meadow Brook."

"Let's have one more picnic on an island!" proposed Nan, a few days before the trip on Lake Romano was to end.

"And a marshmallow roast!" added Dorothy.

"Fine!" cried Bert. "I'll eat all the candies you toast!"

"And I'll help!" added Harry.

"You boys will have to make the fire," Nan said.

"I'll gather wood!" offered Freddie. "And I'll have my little fire engine all ready to put out the blaze, if it gets too big."

"A pail of water will be better," laughed Bert. "Your engine might get going so fast, like it did once, we couldn't stop it."

"I'll sharpen the sticks to put the marshmallows on," offered Harry.

"I wish Will Watson was here to help us eat these," said Nan a little later that afternoon, when the children were having their marshmallow roast on a little island in the lake. "He was a nice boy."

"Yes, and he will be well looked after now," said Mrs. Bobbsey. "Your father had a letter from the miner uncle to-day, saying he was going to make a miner of Will. He gave up the idea of going to sea."

"And will he dig gold?" asked Flossie.

"I suppose so, dear!"

"Oh, I'm going to dig gold when I grow to be a man," said Freddie. "May I have another marshmallow, Nan?" "Yes, little fat fireman," she laughed.

A few days later, after making a trip around the lower end of the lake, the Bobbsey twins started for home, reaching there safely, and having no more trouble with Mr. Hardee and his wire fence.

And so, as they are now safe at home, we shall say good-bye to the Bobbsey twins and their friends.

THE END